A ROCKET FOR THE TOFF

A
ROCKET FOR THE
TOFF

by
JOHN CREASEY

MAGNA PRINT BOOKS
Long Preston, North Yorkshire,
England

British Library Cataloguing in Publication Data

_____

Creasey, John *1908-1973*
   A rocket for the Toff.—Large print ed.
   I. Title

   823′.912(F)   PR6005.R517

   ISBN 0-86009-509-6

First Published in Great Britain 1960

Published in Large Print 1984 by arrangement with Hodder & Stoughton London and the Copyright holder

Photoset in Great Britain by
Dermar Phototypesetting Co., Long Preston, North Yorkshire.

Printed and bound in Great Britain by
Redwood Burn Limited, Trowbridge.

CONTENTS

CHAPTER 1

The Man Who Didn't Arrive

Kate Lowson heard the clear, practical voice of the girl over the airport loud-speaker as she looked out of the window into the soft afterglow which tinged the sky with blues and purples. Above her head, the stars were already showing clearly and the airport lights were on, a shimmering mass of brilliance. Here, on the verandah overlooking the main landing strips were a dozen people, all eagerly waiting the arrival of the aircraft.

'...Flight Number 107, the Strato-Cruiser from New York will arrive on time. It will be cleared at Customs Bay 19. Visitors who are meeting friends off the flight are reminded that they may not enter the Customs Bay or go on to the airfield but are very welcome to wait in the Arrival Hall, where they have all facilities for greeting their friends. The Strato-Cruiser will touch down at'— there was an infinitesimal pause, and then the announcer went on—'seven fifty-one exactly.'

And there was the aircraft.

Kate watched its sleek dark shape against the afterglow, looking only pencil thin from here; it was difficult to believe that there were over a hundred people on board. The cabin had its windows lighted, making it look like a huge, iridescent dragonfly. The aircraft were warming up nearby and there was no sound of the approaching Strato-Cruiser.

A large clock, just above Kate's head, ticked audibly, and the minute hand jerked to seven forty-nine. A man nearby said in a mid-European accent: 'Now it will not long be.' Another man pushed against Kate, said: 'Sorry,' absently, and stared towards the sky. Kate glanced at him. He was young and would have been good-looking but for a flattened nose; she had an impression that he was a boxer. He turned round and looked at her boldly, but without the smile or half

10

smile of the man trying to scrape an acquaintance. She noticed that he had very large, clear brown eyes. Then he turned away, and stood near an attractive girl who was holding an Alsatian on a leash. The girl on the loudspeaker was announcing something else, but Kate's attention had been distracted too much for her to know what it was.

The waiting people drew nearer the window, and Kate moved towards them as the aircraft touched down; it seemed a long way off. She saw the fire tenders and the ambulances waiting, and felt a moment's uneasiness. It would be too dreadful if anything happened to Maurice now. After two years of waiting, sometimes very difficult waiting, that would be the most bitter irony.

A little woman with the mid-European crossed herself and muttered an invocation. Someone said in a rather too affected a voice: 'I'm always glad when they've actually landed, such awful things happen.' No one else spoke. The big dog was straining at a leash and the sound of its heavy breathing was just behind Kate. She glanced round and saw it only a few feet away, its leash now held by the man who had pushed past her; he hadn't held the dog when he had passed before. Then she turned back to the airfield. The aircraft was much nearer now, and looked very large. Men were hurrying towards it as it taxied into position. She pressed against the window, watching as the door opened. After what seemed a long delay, the first passengers appeared and climbed down the steps. The lighting was not good enough for Kate to recognise them, except to notice that the first three were men—the second very tall—the next two passengers were women. It was quite impossible to judge whether Maurice was among the first three.

'*There he is!*' a woman exclaimed. 'You can always tell his limp!'

Kate could just make out the figure of a man who walked with a limp. More and more came out and streamed towards the airport buildings; and she saw them turning towards the left, away from her, so that they were out of sight before they drew close enough for easy recognition.

Well, it wouldn't be long.

The woman who had cried. 'There he is!' was elderly, but her face was radiant and she looked as eager as a young girl.

'How long will it be before he's through Customs?' she asked a man with her.

'It shouldn't be long, dear.'

A young official said: 'With luck, the first passengers will be through in five or six minutes.'

Kate thought: 'I wonder what it will be like, when we actually come face to face.' It was strange that she hadn't asked herself that question until now; it had been just a matter of longing, a kind of taking for granted that when Maurice came home they would be able to pick up exactly where they had left off. Would they? Would *he*? Nothing had changed with her. She had lived in the same flat, known the same people, made hardly a single new acquaintance, whereas Maurice had met hundreds of new acquaintances in completely different, probably exciting, surroundings. His letters hadn't appeared to change in tone, although as the months had passed they had become fewer, for he had become much busier.

She was probably tantalising herself for no reason. Why should he have changed at all?

She saw the way the little group broke up, now that there was nothing to see from the window of the terrace. Most of them herded round the door which led from the Customs Bays, just this side of a long railing. Kate found a position from which she could see every passenger as he or she came out, and from which she would be able to recognise Maurice on the instant. She told herself that the moment she set eyes on him she would know whether things were the same or not.

A very tall man appeared, and she felt sure that it was the second one to leave the aircraft. Her heart began to beat fast. She realised that she was clenching her hands tightly, tried to assure herself that there was absolutely nothing to worry about, that of course they would take up where they had left off.

She heard the panting of the dog again, but this time did not look round,

14

because she felt sure that it was on leash. She stared at two more men who came into the waiting-room, both obviously Americans from the cut of their clothes. Then someone exclaimed sharply, a man shouted: 'Come here!' in a high-pitched tone of alarm. Kate turned her head quickly—and saw the Alsatian leaping at her.

Terror welled up in her.

The dog was actually off the ground, leash trailing behind it, jaws open, white teeth gleaming, a glint in its eyes which heaped terror upon terror. Kate flung her hands up to her face, but on the same instant the dog thumped into her. She lost her balance and went staggering backwards, terror still raging inside her. She thought she heard screaming. She felt herself falling. She bumped her head on the ground, and it made her dizzy, but not dizzy enough to take away the dread. The dog was growling and snarling over her, and she lay on her back with her arms crossed in front of her face; saliva dripped on to her cheeks.

Then, something hit her on the side of the head, and she lost consciousness.

15

* * * *

When she came round, she was still frightened, and still seemed to be struggling for breath. A man was holding her hands firmly, keeping her from clenching her fingers, and someone else was bending over her—a woman with a pale face and wearing a white uniform; a nurse, of course. The nurse was smiling, as if with reassurance, and the man said:

'All right, she's coming round. She'll be all right.'

'I'm terribly sorry,' a man was saying, and his voice seemed to be high-pitched and nervous. 'I'm terribly sorry, I've never known it happen before.'

'That dog ought to be put away,' a man said angrily.

'No, really, I don't think—' protested the one who had said he was sorry.

To Kate, these were a jumble of voices and a curious mixture of faces, one merging into another so that some people seemed to have two noses, two mouths, two chins, four eyes. She felt a cool hand at her forehead, and then realised that she was no longer on the floor, but on a couch. The hallucinations faded. She saw the nurse clearly, as well as the very young man holding her hands, and the man with the flattened nose—who was without the dog now.

'Look here,' he said, 'I'm terribly sorry, but unless the young lady is seriously hurt, I ought to go. My sister and I were meeting some relations we haven't seen for over ten years. She *isn't* seriously hurt, is she?'

'No, she'll be all right,' answered the absurdly young man. 'You'd better leave your name and address, and then I don't see any reason why you shouldn't go. Do you, sergeant?'

Kate hadn't seen the sergeant before. He was in uniform, but not that of a London policeman. He was middle-aged, and seemed to know exactly what he was doing. He was crisp-voiced, too.

'Provided you're quite sure that the young lady isn't seriously hurt, doctor.'

'I'm quite sure.'

'Here's my address,' the broken-nosed man said anxiously. 'I'm sorry I haven't a card.' He was scribbling on a sheet torn

17

from a small notebook. 'Look here, I'll be at home after nine o'clock, nothing would make us go out tonight once we're home. *Is* it all right for me to go?'

He looked at Kate appealingly. He seemed rather earnest and anxious, but there was something about the situation which she didn't quite understand, and which puzzled her. She was feeling a little numbed, but was reassured by the young doctor's words. There was no point in making the owner of the dog stay, of course, but—

Maurice of course! He wasn't here, that was what puzzled her.

She exclaimed: 'But where is he?' and struggled up, and began to look round. Something like panic filled her. The room was almost empty, except for the group near her. A couple was standing by the door, and Kate had the impression that the woman was in tears. Two men in uniform were coming from the passage which led from the Customs Bay. Kate twisted her head round. The young doctor, the nurse, the brown-eyed man with the flattened nose were the only people with her, apart from the sergeant.

'I'm really sorry, but—'

'It's all right for you to go,' said the sergeant formally. 'We will get in touch with you if it becomes necessary.'

Kate said. 'But where—' and broke off, realising what must have happened. She had been lying down in this corner, Maurice had come in, looked round, seen no sign of her, and gone off. It was the most mortifying thing imaginable.

'Now don't get excited,' the young doctor cautioned.

'Excited!' Kate echoed, hopelessly. 'If you only knew—'

Five minutes later she was being escorted to a small office. She felt more herself, except that there was a bump at the side of her head which beat rather painfully, throb, throb, throb all the time. The sergeant was saying: 'I'll have a call put out for Mr Holmes. Unless he's gone by taxi, we'll find him. The terminal bus hasn't left yet.'

He bustled off, and the young doctor offered Kate cigarettes.

'I won't offer you a drink, except coffee,' he said. 'Alcohol wouldn't do your head any good. It was shocking bad luck.' He had a rather casual, nonchalant manner, was not really good-looking, and had only a little downy hair at the front of his head although it was bushy enough at the back. 'And the coffee's on the way.'

'You're very good,' Kate said. She heard a voice over the loudspeaker, but there was not one in this room, and she could not distinguish the words.

'There goes your message,' the doctor declared. 'It's ten to one that you'll find Mr Holmes.'

'How long was I lying there?' demanded Kate. 'It seems incredible that—' she broke off, realising how pointless it was to talk like that.

'About twenty minutes altogether,' the doctor answered. 'And they don't lose a lot of time these days with the Customs. No one was held up for special questioning tonight, I gather. Anyhow, Mr Holmes knows where to find you at home, doesn't he?'

Kate said: 'I suppose he'll go straight to my flat.' But obviously she couldn't be sure, and in any case Maurice would not only be disappointed but would feel badly let down. She had said in her last letter that she would be at the airport, that she couldn't wait to see him.

'He'll know it was unavoidable, anyhow,' the doctor soothed, and then the door opened and a girl appeared, carrying a tray with coffee, lump sugar, and biscuits. She brought this across. The doctor put in three lumps of sugar, stirred it thoroughly into the coffee, and was obviously trying to keep Kate's mind off the waiting. She had nearly finished the hot coffee when the door opened again and the sergeant appeared.

The moment she set eyes on him, Kate felt sure that he had disappointing news.

'He's not on the bus and doesn't appear to be on the airport,' he announced. 'Very sorry about that, miss, but there isn't anything else I can do.'

'I'll tell you what *I'll* do,' declared the doctor. 'I was just going off duty when the call came, and I'm in a heck of a hurry to get to London. I'll get you home almost as soon as Mr Holmes arrives there, if not before.'

21

CHAPTER 2

Home

The doctor's car was small, sleek, shiny, and bright red. The plastic top seemed too small for two people, but when they were inside there was a surprising amount of room. He pressed a self-starter, and a moment later the engine snorted. Smoothly but at a considerable speed they went along the wide roads of the airport, through the tunnel, out on the main road. Lights changed as they reached them, and the car shot forward, rather like a smooth rocket. The doctor sat back, still nonchalant, giving the impression that he was taking life easily. He swerved in and out of traffic, and kept Kate sitting on the edge of her seat; for the first five minutes, she was scared all the time.

He slowed down towards a corner.

'No need to think we'll crash,' he re-assured her. 'I think too much of my young life. These Wasps are deceptive, they work on foam rubber springs.' He glanced at her, smiling pleasantly. His round, pinkish face with its small, snub nose, still gave the impression of youthfulness, and yet the bald patch at the front of his head made him seem quite old. 'Meeting boy friend?' he inquired.

'Yes.'

'How long's he been away?'

'Two years.'

'Has he, b'God!' The doctor looked away from her, as if sensing when the traffic was going to move; it did. From then on, either he drove more slowly or else he managed to ease her fears, for she sat back, quite relaxed; but she almost wished that were not so, because immediately she began worrying about Maurice again. Then a new, disturbing thought entered her head. If she had been unconscious for twenty minutes, he hadn't waited very long, and had made no allowance for the possibility that she had been held up in traffic. If he were as impatient as that, it might be a bad sign.

23

Why *did* she feel that everything was not as it should be?

She knew that it was the tone of Maurice's recent letters—nothing he had actually said, but a kind of pre-occupation, almost a lack of warmth, as if he had been writing as a duty and not because he wanted to. Two years. 'Has he, b'God!' her doctor companion had exclaimed, and she wondered what the expression in his eyes had meant. She tried to tell herself that twenty minutes was a reasonable time—and yet Maurice hadn't even gone off in the terminus bus. He must have hired a taxi.

They neared Hammersmith.

'Where is your place?' asked the doctor, at last.

'Oh, I'm sorry. In Chelsea.'

'That's good. Not far from me, I've a place in Victoria.' He grinned: and grinning his nose looked snubbier and his face looked younger even than before. 'Fulham way best?'

'Yes.'

'We should be at your place in twenty minutes flat from the airport,' the doctor guessed. 'If any taxi gets there before us the driver ought to go to jail. With a bit of luck, you'll be on the doorstep to welcome Mr What's-his-name.' He glanced at her, but she was deliberately looking straight ahead of her, pre-occupied with the fact that Maurice hadn't thought it worth waiting even for twenty minutes.

He had always been a man for punctuality, and she had the same trait. It would be understandable if he felt that to be late after two years' absence was no in-dication that this was an epoch-making meeting for her.

They turned into King's Road, Ful-ham.

'I've a studio flat in Gillivry Street,' Kate explained.

'I know the very street,' the doctor told her. 'Scheduled for demolition to make room for one of those nice, ugly, brown brick boxes, isn't it? Do you paint?'

'No. I—' There was really no need to tell him, but he had been so helpful. 'I have a small business in Knightsbridge.'

'Really?'

'Making and selling hats.'

25

'Well, well!' exclaimed the doctor, and shot a glance at her, grinning again. 'I would have sworn it was millinery, clothes or art. Will you think it impudent if I tell you it's a real pleasure to see someone not only worthy of good clothes but dressed in them?'

Kate was startled into a laugh.

'I knew you would have a kindly nature, too,' the doctor said. 'My name's Kennedy—Mike Kennedy, one of the staff doctors and general factotums at the airport. Yours was the most unusual job I've had to do, I think. You must have fallen down in a queer way.'

'Why?'

'The worst bump's on the side of your head, where you had no protection from your hat.'

As he spoke, Kate remembered being struck on the side of the head after she had fallen. She told Kennedy this, and he hummed a little, remarked again that it was queer, and came to the conclusion that someone had probably gone to her help and fallen over her. Then he turned in Gillivry Street, and Kate said:

'Number 17—just past that lamp post

on the right.'

'Right! Mind a little more advice?' Kennedy went on. 'Don't take any alcohol tonight, treat that bruise and bump with proper respect. It isn't anything serious but it will be tender for a few days. I shouldn't put anything on it, but bathing in cold water won't do it any harm. I shouldn't model any hats for a week, anyhow.' He chuckled as he drew up outside the tall, grey, grimy-terraced house where she had her flat, and she had an impression that he was talking to try to help her over the moment of disappointment. He jumped out and rounded the car to open the door for her. 'You'll probably find Mr Holmes here soon.'

'Yes, I expect I shall,' Kate made herself say, and went on: 'You've been most helpful—thank you very much indeed.'

'Only sorry I couldn't do more,' Dr Kennedy said.

He escorted her to the front door, which was always kept unlocked during the day. He opened it. A flight of stairs covered with red linoleum stretched in front of her, and her head was beating badly enough to make her wish she hadn't to face four such flights. But she turned round and held out her hand.

'Goodbye—and thank you very much again.'

'Oh, forget it,' Dr Kennedy said. He had a firm handclasp, and his smile was still broad.

Kate turned and went into the house, pushing the door closed behind her, partly because she didn't want to be seen walking. She felt so giddy. She clutched the handrail, and had to pull herself up the first few steps. After that she felt steadier, but she had seldom had a worse headache, and her heart was thumping. She stopped at each of three landings, feeling sure that Maurice wasn't here yet; he would have come running down once he heard her. She reached her own landing, and stood holding the rail very tightly. The door was closed and locked, of course.

She let herself in.

"Flat" was hardly the right word for this apartment, which was little more than one huge room with an enormous north window. Leading off on one side were a kitchen and bathroom, each so tiny that there was hardly room to move freely; on the other side was a cubicle which she used as a bedroom. The smallness of the lesser rooms was more than compensated for by the size and proportions of this. The ceiling was quite high, except where it sloped to the window, and she had spent a lot of time and thought on decorating it, in order to please Maurice. One wall, opposite the north window, was in a huge panel of Paris scenes in black and white on a pink background, with grey surrounding it. She was familiar with the décor, the comfortable furniture, all of good quality—none of it extremely modern, none of it old.

She closed the door, went into the bathroom, took out a bottle of aspirins, swallowed three, and then went into the big room and sat down on an upright chair with a high back. She could never remember a worse headache. She leaned back and closed her eyes for fully five minutes, telling herself that she would hear the moment the street door opened, and would recognise Maurice's tread on the first stair. But would she? Two years. *Has he b'God?* Why had Dr Kennedy said that? Why was it difficult to think of the pink-faced man as a doctor? 'My name's Kennedy, Mike Kennedy,' and that seemed exactly the right name for him.

A little chiming clock in the bedroom struck nine.

It was no use telling herself that Maurice had taken all this time to get from the airport; he had left in the taxi, possibly in a huff, and hadn't come straight here. She had booked a room for him at a small Kensington Hotel, near his offices, and he was almost certainly there. Surely he would telephone before long. If he didn't, she would have to, but he could hardly have taken this so badly that he would not even lift a telephone to find out what had happened.

She looked across at the telephone standing on the side of a small pedestal desk with a leather top, and nicely carved walnut legs, imitation Queen Anne type. It was a pale blue telephone, the only colour that really went with the room and was also available from the G.P.O. She began to wish it to ring.

Then she noticed that one of the side drawers was open an inch.

That puzzled her, because being something of a creature of habit, she always made sure that each drawer was closed properly before locking the centre drawer—which in turn locked all the others. She hadn't used the desk today, but had spent most of last evening at it, getting invoices, cheques, letters, and everything to do with her business up-to-date, so that for a few days she would be able to take off as much time as Maurice needed. She remembered closing each drawer last night. Frowning, she stood up and went towards the desk. Her head seemed to lift from her shoulders, and she had to stand still for some seconds. When she went forward again there was an ache in front of her eyes and at the back of her head, but she felt better. She pulled at the drawer, and it came open; it was the one in which she kept her writing paper, bill heads and envelopes. She *must* have been careless. She pulled at the centre drawer and it opened.

Now she felt really alarmed, because she was quite sure that she hadn't left this unlocked. She pulled it out further, and saw that all the contents were out of order. The pens and pencils and little oddments she kept at the front were pushed to one side. A shallow tray of pins and paper clips had been upset. A blotting pad, her address book and her bank statements, all kept in here, were lying in the wrong positions. She left the drawer open, bent down and snatched at the bottom one on the right, where she kept her cash box. There had been upwards of a hundred pounds in the box last night—cash against any emergency, chiefly in case Maurice couldn't get to a bank quickly and needed some.

The cash box was still there. She picked it up, and the lid came back. She saw at a glance that the lock had been forced—light glinted on the brass where it had been broken. She hardly needed to open the inside box, to check that it was empty. Even the stamps, the silver and the few postal orders she kept there were gone. She felt a sense of shock and disbelief, that this should have happened to her. Then she put the cash box on the desk, and opened the other drawers, including the double-depth drawer in which she kept her business files. This did not seem to be touched. She checked the others, then realised almost with a sense of shock that Maurice's letters were gone.

There were ninety-one of them; she had counted them only last night. Ninety-one, eleven of them blue airmail letter forms, most of the others on hotel notepaper from all parts of the United States.

And there wasn't one left.

She made quite sure that she had not put them somewhere else in a fit of absent-mindedness, then left the drawers open and went back to her chair, so shaken that she almost forgot how badly her head was aching. She must send for the police, of course. What a miserable thing to happen, especially tonight! She went back to the table, but instead of calling the police at once dialled the number of the Craddock Hotel. She simply couldn't wait any longer, but had to make sure that Maurice was there.

First a girl, then a man, then another girl spoke to her; and finally, the man said:

'No, Mr Holmes has not registered yet, madam. A room has been reserved for him, it was booked by Miss K. Lowson. Is there any other information I can give you?'

'No,' Kate said. 'No, thank you.' She rang off and stared blankly at the telephone. If she called the police they would be here in a few minutes, and would start asking question after question; if Maurice arrived in the middle of it, there would be an impossible situation. She couldn't bring herself to do it. No one would know when she had discovered the theft, even if it waited until morning it would make little difference.

She could understand anyone taking money, but why should they take Maurice's letters?

And why didn't Maurice telephone? Where *was* he?

* * * *

It was half past ten, and she was almost distracted with the uncertainty, the anxiety and the ache in her head, when the telephone bell rang.

CHAPTER 3

A Certain Mr Rollison

Kate caught her breath as she lifted the telephone and seemed to take a long time to get it to her ear. When she said 'Hallo,' it was as if she had a frog in her throat. She felt a sense of relief, sure that she was hearing from Maurice at last, yet knew a kind of bewilderment, almost dismay, because she could not imagine what he would say, what explanation either of them could give.

A man whose voice she only vaguely recognised said: 'Is that Miss Lowson?'

'Yes.' She tried to keep her voice steady.

'I just rang up to find out if the missing lover had turned up, and how your head is,' the man said, and Kate realised belatedly who it was. 'Mike Kennedy here.'

'Oh,' Kate said; and for a moment could not bring herself to go on. Kennedy must think that she was a helpless fool. 'Oh, I—I thought it would be Mr Holmes.'

'Did he turn up?'

Suddenly, she was eager to talk to Kennedy, and tell him everything. She found the words pouring out, even though she reminded herself once or twice that if she didn't stop he would think she was the most garrulous woman he had ever met. She felt a little light-headed, that was the truth. At least he listened patiently and without interruption, until at last she said:

'...I can't imagine where he is, and I can't imagine why anyone should want to take his letters. I can understand the money, of course, but the letters—' she broke off.

'Puzzling and peculiar,' Kennedy agreed. 'I suppose he was *on* that plane.'

'Of course he was!'

'Did you ask at the airport?'

She had not, had simply inquired where Maurice's plane would arrive. He had told her what time he was leaving

New York, given the flight number—107. She hadn't actually checked to find out if his name was among the passengers.

'So you didn't,' said Kennedy, brightly. 'How about it if I call them and check—I know the people concerned and I can get it without a lot of holding on.'

'Will you?' She was really grateful.

'Of course.'

'But if he'd missed the aircraft he would have cabled me,' Kate said, in sudden alarm.

'You've got a point there,' agreed Kennedy, 'but I may as well make sure. I don't want to be an alarmist, but there's always a possibility of an accident in New York—or else someone might have forgotten to send a cable for him. I'll check, and call back in five minutes or so. When did you last have any aspirins?'

'Soon after I came in.'

'How's the head?'

'Not very good, I'm afraid.'

'What you need is a good night's sleep,' declared Kennedy. 'We'll have to fix it. I'll ring off now.' She heard his telephone being hung up, and moved back to the upright chair, so that she could rest the back of her head against it. She wondered, a little vaguely, why anyone should take as much trouble as Mike Kennedy was taking, but her main preoccupation was with Maurice. Kennedy had brought an obvious possibility into the open, and with it there was a fear which had been there all the time. If Maurice had been hurt in New York it would explain everything, too. She felt sure that there had been no slip up over a cable; he would not trust anyone else to send an important message. She pressed her hands against her forehead, got up restlessly, went into the kitchen, and put a kettle on a low gas; it would take ten minutes or so to boil. She went back, walking slowly, knowing that Kennedy was right; she would not really feel herself again until she had slept soundly. But what chance was there of going to sleep?

Why did everything take so *long*?

She was waiting for it intently, but when the bell rang again, it startled her. She leaned forward and snatched up the receiver.

'Kate Lowson speaking.'

'Hallo, Kate Lowson,' greeted Kennedy, but the tone of his voice did nothing to raise her spirits. 'At least I've one kind of good news for you. Maurice Holmes was on the plane. He's on the manifest, his luggage was checked and taken away, and the Customs chaps ticked him off their list after he'd been through Passport Control. There's no doubt that he reached London Airport. Er—was he expecting you?'

Kate made herself say: 'Yes, of course. He's not at his hotel, either.'

'If it were daytime we could check his office or wherever he'd be likely to report,' mused Kennedy, 'but that will have to wait until the morning. What about his relations?'

'He has no close relations.' Kate hesitated, then went on: 'His only close relation was an uncle, Uncle Jerry, who died about two months ago. He has a cousin whom I've never met.' Again, she found it easy to talk to Mike Kennedy, and yet had a feeling that she talked too much. 'I can't understand it, but I expect there will be a message from him soon.'

'Checked his hotel more than once?'

'No.'

'You said it was the Craddock, didn't you?' said Kennedy. 'I know it slightly, they've a cheerful little snack bar, one of the best corners in London for beer and oysters—champagne if you prefer it. Did you have dinner before you left home this evening?'

'No.' It was hardly worth saying that she had expected to have dinner with Maurice.

'Tell you what—you get yourself some food, your head is bound to be bad if you're hungry,' Kennedy declared. 'I'll call the Craddock Hotel, check again, and then come round and give you a dose of a sedative to keep you quiet all night. That's what you need more than anything else.'

'No, really, I—'

'Doctor's orders,' said Kennedy firmly, and rang off.

After a minute or two, Kate got up, went into the kitchen, took out eggs and bacon, and began to cook them; suddenly she realised how ravenously hungry she was. She kept the kitchen door shut so that the odour of frying bacon would not be too noticeable in the big room, made herself some toast, and ate at the corner of the tiny table. She finished the meal in twenty minutes, and felt much better, although her head still ached. She ran a comb through her hair, very gingerly at the spot where her head was tender, brushed off her shoulders, and put on a little more lipstick. Sitting in front of the mirror she saw that her eyes were slightly bloodshot; there seemed to be dark patches under them. If Maurice walked into this room this very moment, he would think she had aged ten years instead of two. She looked nearer forty than thirty.

Then she heard footsteps on the stairs coming up to this apartment, and when she reached the big room, she realised that not one man but two were coming up. She hesitated, near the door. It might be Maurice. It might be Maurice *and* this Dr Kennedy, who might have found Maurice at the hotel! She did not know what to do, and told herself that she was behaving like a child. Yet her breath was coming very fast when at last there was a ring at the door bell.

Could Kennedy and Maurice be together?

'Coming,' she found herself calling, as she always did to Maurice, and fumbled as she slid back the door knob, she was so anxious to see him.

It wasn't Maurice.

It was Kennedy and a stranger.

Kate was so acutely disappointed that she didn't speak, just backed inside the room to allow Kennedy to come in first. He looked pink and young, and a trick of the light made him seem completely bald. The other man was taller, and quite startlingly handsome—rather like someone she knew. A film star, perhaps; there was a Rex Harrison kind of look about him. He was immaculately dressed in one of those suits which seemed to be made of a material poured over the body and made to fit like a skin at the shoulders. His dark hair curled a little, and had a few specks of grey at the temples.

'Hallo, Kate Lowson,' greeted Kennedy, as if he had known her all his life. 'I've brought a friend along, a man you might say specialises in mysteries. Richard

43

Rollison, meet Kate possibly for Katherine Lowson. I've told Rolly that we aren't exactly lifelong friends,' Kennedy went on brightly, 'and I've given him an outline of the situation.'

Kate exclaimed: 'Rollison!'

'Good evening, Miss Lowson,' the stranger greeted, in a pleasant voice which seemed a little deeper than most men's. 'I'm sorry you're having this anxiety, and if I can help I gladly will.'

She stared at him as if at a ghost.

'Spotted in one, Rolly,' declared Kennedy. 'A certain Mr Rollison has been identified as the Toff. That right, Kate?' He was further in the room, glancing at the desk with the open drawers, and Rollison glanced at it, too. 'You certainly didn't lose much time.'

Kate said, almost sharply: 'Of course I know the Toff, surely everyone—' she broke off, seeing Rollison smile. He was smiling only at her, and gave her an unexpected feeling of confidence. She had read of him over the years, for he was frequently in the headlines—especially those of the more sensational Sunday newspapers. He was known to be consulted by the police, and if she wanted to talk about him rather cynically—as most people talked about him at some time or other—she would have called him the "aristocratic private eye". No one had ever matched the word "aristocratic" better than this man. His complete ease of movement and of manner seemed to suit the word perfectly.

'May I have a look at the desk which was forced open?' he asked, and moved towards it. 'Is this the one?'

'Yes,' Kate said. 'But why—?'

'Let the great man get to work, you can ask questions afterwards,' Kennedy said. 'There's no need for alarm, I just thought he'd do you more good than any doctor.' He was touching her right hand lightly, and they stood together and watched as Rollison bent over the desk, then knelt down on one knee and studied the governor lock, which controlled all the drawers. He did not touch it with his fingers, but took a knife out of his pocket, opened it at a kind of skewer blade, poked a little, then pushed the drawer in and pulled it out with the blade. He glanced round.

'Very neat and a thoroughly professional job,' he announced. 'I shouldn't expect to find any prints here, but he might have left some in other parts of the room. Mike says that only the money and the letters are missing.'

'Yes, that's right.'

'What about jewellery?'

'I'm wearing the only jewellery I possess.'

'May as well see if the chap realised that,' said Rollison easily. 'Which is the bedroom?'

'It's hardly a bedroom,' Kate began apologetically, 'it's just a cubby hole, but there is a dressing-table.'

She stood in the doorway, watching Rollison as he examined the dressing-table. She could see his profile clearly; it was so handsome she didn't quite believe this was real. He seemed intent only on what he was doing, and that was somehow surprising. She had read of him as a fabulous, almost a legendary figure, glamorous, daredevil, touched with a kind of detective genius; somehow she had never pictured him as a man who would take such pains as this.

46

He straightened up.

'I shouldn't think it's been touched, except by you,' he said. 'I can see your fingerprints and some marks on a light dusting of powder, but no extensive marks like there are on the desk. Is this him, by the way?'

He picked up a photograph in a leather pedestal frame of Maurice, smiling, dark-haired, preciously familiar.

'Yes,' Kate answered.

'He looks as if he knows what he wants,' Rollison remarked lightly, and changed the subject. 'How much money would you say there was?'

'Just over a hundred pounds.'

'Any keys or securities?'

'No—I keep the keys in my handbag, and a duplicate set at the shop, where I'm more likely to need them.'

'Can you imagine any reason why a thief would want to take those letters?' asked Rollison. Quite suddenly he smiled as broadly and as warmly as Kennedy, and she had a sense of the extreme likeableness of this man. His eyes gleamed. 'Could there be anything particularly interesting even to a student of love

47

letters?'

'No, I don't think so,' she said, flushing a little.

'Maurice Holmes didn't write in purple phrases?'

Kate found herself laughing. 'Neither of us writes in purple phrases. I suppose —well, they were affectionate letters, that's all.'

'Did the letters give you any information which wouldn't be likely to be found anywhere else?'

'I can't imagine what you're getting at,' Kate answered.

'Let me make myself clearer,' said Rollison, as if musingly. 'Could either you or he conceivably be blackmailed if anyone else knew about the letters?' As she began to say "no", emphatically, he went on: 'Let me finish, then one "no" will cover the lot! Did he give away any business secrets or trade secrets? Was he inclined to tell you too much about his business?'

'No,' she answered quickly, and then laughed again, because that was so obviously the reply Rollison expected. Kennedy was smiling, too. 'I can't think

48

of anything in the letters which could possibly interest anyone but Maurice and me.'

'It could be that the thief thought there might be something—er—dare I say juicy in them? You know what a kick some people get out of prying into other people's affairs,' Kennedy said.

'I know very well,' Rollison answered, and I also know that the chap who did this job took his time. There's no evidence of haste about anything he did. He didn't go into the bedroom, so he wasn't simply looking for any valuables he could find. He went straight to the desk, but didn't touch any of Miss Lowson's millinery business papers. The money was easy and at hand, so he would have been a fool to leave it behind and make it obvious that he wasn't simply after money. What we've got to find out is why he should be interested in the letters.' He was looking straight into Kate's eyes, and she had a feeling that she wasn't going to like what he said next. It was some time before he went on, in that deep and very pleasant voice, the kind which seemed to make it clear that he meant exactly what he said. 'If it's true that the letters could only interest Mr Holmes or you, and you didn't take them, then—'

'Did *he?*' Kennedy asked, explosively.

'I was going to ask, did Mr Holmes have a key?' asked Rollison. 'There's no sign that the front door was forced. Did he have one?'

Kate wanted to say: "It's ludicrous, it's ridiculous, you're behaving like a fool!"—but the fact remained that Maurice did have a key to the apartment.

CHAPTER 4

Missing?

When Richard Rollison first saw Kate Lowson, he thought: 'She's really something out of the ordinary,' and he could understand why Mike Kennedy was so fascinated by her; "fascinated" was the only word that would explain Mike's attitude towards her. Rollison knew him fairly well, liked what he knew, and was quite sure that Mike did not wear his heart on his sleeve; certainly he did not lose his head over every girl with a handsome face and a figure that would not have shamed Marilyn Monroe. True, this young woman—she was in her late twenties, Rollison judged—was dark, but she had a curiously smooth and unblemished complexion, and her eyes were remarkably fine, a chestnut brown in colour, although they were a little bloodshot.

As she stood staring at him, his question about the key still unanswered, he could see that she was bewildered and distressed.

At that stage he had no idea at all whether this was a case which either did or should interest him. Mike had telephoned when he, Rollison, had been taking an evening off and was in his Mayfair flat alone. Mike was a persuasive young man. 'It's got all the makings of a proper puzzle,' he had urged, 'and the woman in the case has got everything. Be a gallant, Rolly, like your reputation.'

For once, the irrepressible Mike was silent now.

Then Kate answered: 'Yes, Maurice had a key, but it's quite absurd to suggest that he came on here and—and took those letters away. I—I mean, why on earth should he? Why should anyone?'

'It's what we're trying to discover,' said Rollison. He wondered whether she could be keeping anything back, and the one certain way to find out was to make her angry; in anger, he would probably find out what was really in her mind. So he went on, as if mildly: 'Were there any promises of marriage in the letters, for instance?'

At first, she had been rather flushed, but the colour receded, and the resulting paleness made her eyes seem even brighter than before—feverishly bright and angry.

'If you mean, would he take the letters so as to go back on his promise of marriage, that is an unforgivable thing to suggest,' she said coldly. 'There really is no need to make such suggestions.'

Rollison saw that Mike was also taken aback, and the girl gave the impression that she wished they would go, that she wished they had never come; but she did not give the impression that she was hiding anything.

'Miss Lowson,' Rollison said, more briskly, 'we have a problem, and there's no point in being too touchy or sentimental about it. Mr Holmes hasn't turned up. That could be of his own free will, or it could be what we know as "missing". If someone else made him—or persuaded him—to go off, the quicker we can be sure the better. There are indications that he might have been persuaded—indications that your fall wasn't quite the accident it seemed. I'm sorry if I seem to impute unpleasant motives— in fact I'm simply trying to get at the truth.'

He liked the way she reacted, and the change in her expression told him that she admitted the sense in what he said. Then she gave a frown which showed fresh alarm.

'What do you mean, the accident wasn't what it seemed?'

'There is a possibility that the dog was deliberately released to jump at you,' Rollison said. 'Alsatians can be trained to strict obedience, and everything we know about this case suggests that a trained dog leapt at you, knocked you down, and stood over you without making any attempt to harm you. That wasn't characteristic of a badly behaved dog, or one out of control. There was never any fear that it would maul you—isn't that right, Mike?'

'It's what the people at the airport said,' answered Kennedy. Rollison saw him flush, and his engaging grin couldn't disguise his slight embarrassment. 'As a matter of fact, Kate Lowson, after leaving you here I went back to the airport and had a chat with the sergeant and the others on duty,' he went on. 'The sergeant you saw is ex-RAF, and knows something about trained dogs. He said this one behaved just like that. Then there was that bump on the side of your head—we thought you'd been kicked. It wasn't a really powerful kick, but there is just one spot on the head where a sharp blow will always make you unconscious for twenty minutes or so. Someone caught you right on that solar plexus of the cranium. It could have happened by accident, but there's an even chance that it was intentional.'

'But why on earth should—?' began Kate.

Watching her closely, Rollison realised that she had a quick and lively mind; she broke off because she realised what her visitors were driving at. He did not push her, and glanced at Kennedy, adjuring him not to interrupt. Kate's eyes narrowed, and very slowly she shook her head.

'It can't be true. You mean that someone actually knocked me out to make sure that I wasn't able to meet Maurice.'

'It could have happened,' Kennedy said, uneasily.

Kate looked at Rollison.

'Do you seriously think that it did?'

'Only that it could, so far. The thief was in this flat a little while before you, I'd say, no dust settled after he'd made marks, as far as I can see. I imagine he was here within an hour of your returning. It's quite possible that if it wasn't Mr Holmes, then it was someone who took the key from him. Would you recognise this man with the Alsatian again?'

'Vividly,' Kate answered.

"Here's the kind of witness I like," Rollison thought, and asked: 'How would you describe him?'

'He was about five feet ten, rather broad-shouldered, had dark hair cut very short at the sides, a rather large nose which seemed as if it were flattened, full lips—a short upper lip, I think—and a rather square chin. His voice was much higher-pitched than I expected.'

'Bang on the nose,' applauded Kennedy. 'I couldn't put it better in a thousand words.'

'Did you see anyone with him?' asked Rollison.

'No. He talked about having a sister with him, and presumably she looked after the dog at first,' answered Kate. She stood very still, looking into Rollison's eyes, and he could guess what was coming next. 'Mr Rollison, do you think that my fiancé is in danger?'

'He could be. Do you know of any reason why he should be?'

'No.'

'Was his business in America of any great importance?'

Kate said, raising her hands as if helplessly: 'Well, it was to him—he's been negotiating the sale of motor cars and arranging the distribution of spare parts and service goods for a new Malling car,' she answered. 'But I can't imagine that would matter very much to anyone. Hundreds of people knew what he was doing, and worked with him.' She gave Rollison the impression that she was trying hard to think of some reasonable explanation.

'I'll talk to Malling Motors in the morning,' Rollison promised. 'Meanwhile—'

'Bed for you, and I've brought these pills,' put in Kennedy more heartily. 'Take two. You'll sleep soundly for eight hours and wake up fit to create a dozen new hats.' He was a natural clown. 'Can you run to some hot milk to wash them down?'

'Yes. Mr Rollison,' Kate went on, 'will you try the Craddock Hotel again?'

'I arranged for a telephone message to come here if he turned up there,' Rollison told her. 'You needn't worry that the normal things will be left undone. We'll go to the airport, find out the names of everyone on duty, and find out if Mr Holmes was seen speaking to anyone else. It shouldn't be difficult to check.' He glanced at the bedroom door. 'Is that photograph on your dressing-table the only one you have?'

'No—I've another one.'

'May we take it?'

'Yes, of course,' Kate answered, and

58

pressed a hand against her forehead. 'You really think that he is in danger, don't you?'

'I only think it would be worth finding out where he is,' Rollison said re-assuringly. He glanced at Kennedy, who had shaken two small tablets on to the palm of his right hand. 'We may want your help in the morning, Miss Lowson. Can you take time off?'

'I can give you as much time as you need,' answered Kate. 'Are you sure there's nothing I can do now?'

'According to Mike here, if you don't get a good night's sleep you won't be any use to anyone in the morning,' Rollison answered.

'I suppose you're right,' said Kate, and held out her hand for the tablets.

* * * *

Ten minutes later, Mike Kennedy closed the door of the apartment quietly, yet made the latch click, then turned to Rollison and asked eagerly: 'Well, what do you think of her?' He stood facing Rollison, as if determined that neither of them should take another step without Rollison's opinion being voiced.

'Not bad,' said Rollison. 'Not bad at all.'

'Not *bad?* Don't be a clot, she's a pippin!' When Rollison didn't answer at once, Kennedy went on rather anxiously: 'You don't think she's been fooling me, do you?'

'Shouldn't think so,' said Rollison, and he meant that. 'It's a curious problem, though. How many of the people on duty when Flight 107 came in are likely to be there now?'

'Most of them—they'd be the six to two o'clock shift. I will say,' went on Kennedy, 'that when you tackle a job, you tackle it. My car, or yours?'

'Mine,' answered Rollison, firmly. They reached the street, where Kennedy's shiny midget and Rollison's magnificent Rolls-Bentley stood one behind the other. 'You may kill yourself when you're on your own. Before we start, though, I want to make a telephone call—I ought to tell Jolly that I'll be late. What about your car? Will you leave it here or find a garage?'

'Why don't I nip home in it? You can telephone from the corner, I saw a kiosk there, and by the time you're through I'll be nearly as far as King's Road, even walking. You can pick me up there, by the Town Hall. Right?'

'Right,' said Rollison, obligingly.

He watched Kennedy drive off, at a curiously silent speed, then looked up at the top floor of Kate Lowson's house. Her apartment was at the back, and one of the windows was visible from here. He went to the other side of the road, and saw a glow from the top of the house. It went out, almost on that instant, so she had left the big room. He slid into his car and drove to the corner, parked some distance from the telephone kiosk, and walked quietly back to the street and peered along it, he saw no one. He opened the heavy door of the kiosk, put in his coins, and dialled his own Gresham Terrace flat. The bell had hardly started to ring before he was answered:

'This is the Honourable Richard Rollison's residence.'

'Hallo, Jolly,' Rollison said briskly. 'This job isn't at all uninteresting, and it will stop me from getting rusty if nothing else. There's an outside chance that it might be wise to watch Miss Lowson's apartment. Will you telephone Ebbutt, get a couple of his chaps laid on, and then come here until they can take over?'

'Immediately, sir,' answered Jolly. 'Is there any special thing to look out for?'

'I'd just like to be sure she doesn't have any visitors,' Rollison said.

He rang off on Jolly's assurances, hesitated, then walked to the spot from which he could see along Gillivry Street. He stood staring along it for fully five minutes, not sure why he felt on edge, yet anxious to make sure that the girl was not left unattended.

Then he saw two men walk along the street and turn into Number 17, or a house very close by. One of them went into the house; the other stayed outside.

CHAPTER 5

Intent to Murder?

Why should a man stand outside there, as if on guard? Rollison asked himself.

He heard no sound, and realised suddenly that he had not heard either of the men. They had walked on rubber soles, making no noise, and even the closing of the street door had been done softly. He turned into the street, walking on the other side of the road. He saw the man by the porch staring towards him, but did not check his speed or look towards the man. Number 17 was between two street lamps and there was very little light. Rollison passed the man, and out of the corner of his eyes saw that the other was wearing a trilby hat pulled low over his forehead so that it was difficult to see his face. He made no attempt to conceal himself.

He was watching Rollison closely.

Rollison strode on, as if he had not noticed the man, and drew level with him. He could imagine the other's relief, could imagine that very moment when he relaxed. And in that moment, Rollison spun round and darted across the road. He needed several seconds' start—and his tactics so startled the other that he won them. As he reached the pavement the man was turning and leaping desperately for the door. He reached it, and pushed it open as Rollison caught him with in a flying tackle.

The man crashed against the door, and it banged back. Rollison knocked his knee painfully, winced, but did not let it put him off. He knelt over his victim, who was struggling desperately to get up. Only a pale blur of his face and the whiteness of his teeth showed. Rollison thrust his right hand over the writhing mouth, stopped the man from calling out, then crooked the fingers of his left hand round his throat. The man could hardly breathe because of Rollison's knee on his chest, but he kept struggling, and it was difficult for Rollison to be

64

sure whether anyone was coming down the stairs.

The man's struggles grew weaker, and his chest heaved less.

Rollison relaxed his grip, and listened intently. Feeling sure that no one was coming down, he glanced at the face of the man on the floor.

'We'll have a little chat later,' he said. He bent further down, lifted the man's head in his hands, and banged it sharply on the stone step. He felt the body go limp. 'That should put you to sleep for twenty minutes or so,' he went on, 'but I'd better make sure who you are.' He slid his hands into the other's pockets, and took out the usual oddments—and the unusual .32 automatic pistol from the hip pocket. 'I wonder if you've a licence,' he said musingly. His words were slow, but his movements were swift. He took out a wallet and some letters, thrust these into his own pocket, then straightened up. He dragged the other inside, closed the door, and went to the foot of the stairs. He heard no sound. He went up to the first landing, where a low-powered electric lamp gave a dim yellow glow. He could see nothing and hear nothing. He hurried up the next flight of stairs, watching every landing and every shadow cautiously, knowing that the man who had come in here might have heard the struggle downstairs and be waiting ready to pounce or shoot—or might be in Kate Lowson's flat.

* * * *

Kate thought, in a strangely calm mood, that Dr Kennedy had really given her a drug which worked wonders. Five minutes after taking it and a glass of hot milk, her anxiety seemed to ease. She wondered if he had given her not only a sleeping but a tranquillising drug. Probably it was as well if he had. It was peculiar, though, to feel that she ought to be so anxious about Maurice, and at the same time that she could forget about him, and rest.

She yawned.

Only habit made her do the odds and ends of chores she usually did; washing up the cup and saucer, setting out a tea tray for the morning, pulling back the curtains. She was yawning more when she got into bed. She turned off the light, sure that she would be asleep in five minutes. There was no sound, and it was very dark up here. It took her longer to get to sleep than she expected, but she was completely relaxed and free from any sense of alarm; that was the main thing.

She heard a sound outside.

It did not worry, only puzzled her. She often heard sounds. There was a couple in the flat immediately beneath who were late birds, and who usually came home in the early hours. There were the creaking noises of the floorboards. There were the unexplained noises of the night. Yet this sound made Kate more alert than she had been, and she was more annoyed because it had stopped her from going off to sleep than frightened.

She heard the sound again.

What *was* it?

She listened intently, lying on her back so that neither ear was muffled, but the position wasn't comfortable, because of the bruises. She stared at the door. There was no sound for at least a minute, and she began to think that she had been imagining things when she heard an unmistakable creak not far from the door.

She thought: *Perhaps it's Maurice.*

She lay still, her heart beating faster than it had a few minutes before, and yet she had no great feeling of alarm or excitement. If it were Maurice, why had he come in so furtively? Who else had a key? She had a peculiar feeling—that she ought to be much more alarmed than she was.

Then she heard the handle of the door turn; it always squeaked a little. Any other night, she would have been terrified, but that induced calm was upon her. She eased herself up on one elbow, and called clearly:

'Maurice! Is that you?'

There was no answer at first.

'Maurice, is—' she began.

'*Yes!*' she heard, vaguely. '*Yes, Kate.*'

She hitched herself up in bed, quite convinced in her own mind that it was Maurice, not knowing what to say or how to greet him. There was no sense in the way she was behaving, but there seemed nothing she could do about it.

She waited for the door to open. When it did, the room beyond was in darkness of course. She could just make out the shape of a man's head and shoulders as she stretched out to switch on the bedside light.

'Don't put on a light!' he called in a whisper.

Maurice seldom whispered, but there seemed nothing remarkable about the furtiveness now. He had missed her—perhaps actually avoided her—at the airport, and now he had crept up here late at night. Could he have been here before, for those letters? What could he possibly want from them? What could anyone want?

The door opened wider, and she whispered back:

'No one will see us. Why mustn't we have the light?'

'Just a minute,' he urged.

She felt quite sure of one thing; he was scared. She heard his heavy, agitated breathing. He was moving so slowly, too, as if he feared that there was someone else in the room—or else, someone just on his heels. Could that be it? Was he being followed? There was no real sense of urgency in her mind, she simply wanted to know the answers.

He was at the foot of the bed when she realised for the first time that it wasn't Maurice. This man wasn't tall enough.

All the false calm vanished. She opened her mouth to scream, but her voice died. She raised her hands in front of her, and the man flung himself forward. But for one thing, she would have had no chance at all to save herself. The one thing was the narrow gap between the bed and the wall; the man could not be as swift as he wanted to. Kate struck out at him, and her nails scratched his hand. She tried to snatch up the lamp from the dressing-table, but it slipped and fell. She thrust her hands out again, to fend him off, and felt the nails of her right hand scratch his face; then suddenly he was upon her, pushing her back on to the bed, hands groping for her throat.

She screamed.

His hands fastened round her throat with awful tightness, and she knew that he was going to kill her.

She could not see him clearly; there was only a kind of glow at his eyes and a whiteness at his mouth. The pressure of his hands was awful. She felt as if his whole weight was crushing down on her, knew that he was standing at the side of the bed and bearing down on her throat. Her lungs seemed to be filled with leaden weights. There were strange and unfamiliar lights at her eyes. There was pain in her head, sharp, excruciating flashes of pain.

Then a different light came on, and the pressure eased. She felt herself flop down on her pillows, and began to struggle for breath.

* * * *

Rollison heard Kate Lowson scream as he reached the door of her flat. It was a muted scream, and seemed to be cut off immediately—no one else in the house was likely to have heard it, but he was standing outside the door with a picklock in his hand, and a torch shining on to the lock. As the scream came, he thrust his hand on the handle and pushed the door—and it swung open.

Beyond was darkness but for the grey outline of the big windows. He heard gasping and struggling coming from the bedroom. He sprang towards the door, flashing his pencil torch until the beam shone on the light switch. He pressed this down, and saw the man bending over the bed. He could just see the girl's bare shoulders, and knew exactly what the man was doing. He raised his right hand and brought the side of it down on the man's neck, and as he did so, gripped the other's right shoulder with his own hand, to stop him from falling on the girl.

The man twisted round.

The girl was struggling for breath.

Somehow, the man managed to kick at Rollison, and caught him painfully on the knee which he had bruised downstairs. Rollison winced, and slackened his grip, but he was in the narrow space between the bed and the wall, and the other had no chance to push past him. He remembered that the man downstairs had had a gun—and he saw the man's right hand moving towards his pocket. He thrust his own hand forward to try and push the killer off his balance, but the space restricted all freedom of movement.

He saw a knife flash in the other's hand.

He knew from the speed of the movement that he was dealing with an expert. The knife came stabbing towards him, pointing slightly upwards; if it struck home, it would rip into his stomach. Yet he could not twist round or back away. He brought up his right knee. He felt sharp pain as the knife caught the knee, but the blade was deflected, and the other had concentrated all his effort into that blow and was lurching forward. Rollison brought his left fist up in a slashing uppercut, and jarred his knuckles on the hard jaw. The man's head jerked backwards, and his eyes rolled.

Kate Lowson was still gasping for breath.

Rollison had the pain at his knee, and the reaction from that moment of fear. He backed away. At least the girl was all right. She was lying back on the pillows, her face grey, her hair very dark against the white. The man had collapsed in a curious crouching position, one arm crooked on the bed preventing him from falling, head lolling forward. Rollison reached the end of the bed, where he had more freedom of movement, and glanced round at the door. He heard and saw nothing. He needed a few minutes' respite, and limped towards the door to make sure all was well. No one was coming up, but he reminded himself that the man he had attacked might have come round more quickly than he anticipated, so there was the risk of another attack.

His knee felt warm and sticky.

He pulled up his trouser leg and saw a wound about two inches long, on the right side of the knee cap. It wasn't deep enough to do any permanent damage, but it could be stiff and sore for a few days. He limped to the kitchen, wrung out a towel, wiped the blood off the knee, then tied the handkerchief round it so that he had more comfort when moving. All the time, he was on the alert for any sound outside or in the bedroom.

He heard only the girl, breathing very heavily, and went to her again. The man was in exactly the same position, and Kate Lowson was beginning to hitch herself up in bed. She had a little colour, but her eyes looked glassy.

'Take it easy,' Rollison advised. 'There's no hurry and nothing more to worry about.' He leaned forward, gripped the unconscious man's wrist, hauled him to his feet, and dragged him bodily along by the bed, out of the little cubicle, and into the big room. He stood him in front of a large armchair, then pushed him into it. The man flopped down.

He was dark-haired, youngish, about five feet ten—and his nose was flattened and pushed to one side. There was little doubt that this was the man who had released the Alsatian at the airport.

As he realised that, Rollison heard another sound, of someone coming stealthily up the stairs.

CHAPTER 6

More Facts

Rollison crept to the door.

He had left it ajar, and knew that whoever was coming up would see the light on. He stepped just behind the door as the newcomer reached the landing, still moving very stealthily. It might be the man from below. It might be his own man, Jolly. It might possibly be Kennedy. Rollison stood waiting, right knee stinging more than aching, thoughts concentrated on the unknown outside. He did not think there was much risk that the man with the flattened nose would come round in time to take any part in the next move, but it was impossible to be certain.

The door began to open.

Flat Nose was sitting in front of it, so that no one could miss him.

There was a moment's pause, and then Kennedy exclaimed *sotto voce*: 'Good God!'

Rollison eased himself away from the wall, and said heavily: 'You took your time, didn't you?' But when Kennedy stepped swiftly inside and stared at him, Rollison was smiling. 'Thanks.'

'What is it?' Kennedy almost squeaked. 'The place looks like a battlefield. Is—God!' He thrust the door back with a bang, and streaked for the bedroom, and Rollison saw him pull up short at the foot of Kate's bed. Rollison ran a hand over the back of his head, able to relax, if only for a few moments. He went into the kitchen again, rinsed his face, and was drying himself on a towel when Kennedy appeared at the bedroom door, saying:

'The swine tried to strangle her.'

'So it seems.'

'Seems be damned!' barked Kennedy. 'He did. Her throat's swollen and puffy from the bruising. I'd like to—' he took a step towards the unconscious man, as if would gladly strangle him.

'None of this eye-for-an-eye business,' Rollison said. 'We leave that to the law.

77

How is she?'

'Eh?'

'How is Kate?'

'Er—she's all right. Pretty badly shaken up, but—Rolly, what the hell happened?'

'You were telling me.'

'Why the heck should anyone want to kill *her?*'

'It would certainly be a waste,' Rollison agreed. He took out cigarettes and proffered them. Kennedy took one, lit it, and began to puff to hard. Then he glanced down at Rollison's leg, and exclaimed:

'There's blood on your shoe!'

'Our Mr Flat Nose meant business all right,' said Rollison. 'The knife's by the side of the bed, I'll get it in a minute. Did you see the chap downstairs?'

'Yes,' answered Kennedy, huskily. 'I couldn't understand why you hadn't turned up, toddled along to your car, and when I didn't see you there, decided I'd better come here. Good thing you hadn't locked that street door. The chap downstairs was just coming round, and when I bent over him he tried to butt me in the head, so I clouted him one to make sure that he didn't get up too soon. Was that all right?'

'Perfect,' agreed Rollison. 'And Jolly should be along here soon.' He paused, drew deeply on his cigarette, and added: 'What we have to decide is how soon to call the police.'

'Ah, yes,' said Kennedy. 'A case for the coppers, all right.' He smoothed his hand over his forehead, and there was a note of anxiety in his voice. 'I'm glad I called you in, Rolly, and even more glad you wouldn't leave Kate on her own. If it hadn't been for that she would be dead by now. That's a pretty shattering thought.' He kept rubbing his head, very slowly. 'I never could stomach murder. Air crashes and car crashes are all part of the day's work, but there's something about cold-blooded wilful murder—' he hesitated, but went on vehemently: 'What gets into a man? I mean, if there was just one chap and he hated Kate's guts, you could understand it, but here are a pair of them, ready to kill. You used the word professionals before, didn't you? They're professionals all right, and it's the first time I've come up against any. Good job it isn't *your* first time.' He hesitated again but soon went on talking, as if he could not stop himself. 'What made you come back? Is this what they call your sixth sense? All I can say is, it's uncanny. Thank God!'

At last, he stopped.

'Jolly would call it subconscious deductive reasoning,' Rollison observed, and grinned. Then he raised his voice for no apparent reason, and said again: 'The question is, when shall we send for the police?'

He glanced at the big armchair, where Flat Nose sat unmoving.

Kennedy started to speak, but only whispered: 'Oh, I get you. You want him to hear.' Rollison stood up, his knee sharply painful. He limped as he went to the door and looked into the tiny bedroom. Kate Lowson was sitting upright, with a woollen wrap around her shoulders. She had her eyes half closed, but the moment Rollison appeared, she opened them wider. Kennedy was just behind Rollison. 'Kate,' Rollison said, 'is there anything at all you know that you haven't told us?'

'Absolutely nothing,' she answered, in a bewildered way. 'I—I just can't help you, Mr Rollison. I can't help what you do, either, I feel—as if I can't keep awake any longer. There are a hundred things I want to do, but I just can't keep awake.'

'Those *tablets!*' exclaimed Kennedy. 'I'd forgotten. My lord, you must have will-power enough for a dozen if you can keep awake after a couple of those! Before you drop off, Kate, Rolly wants to know if there's any reason at all why you don't want us to tell the police everything?'

'I don't mind what you tell anybody,' Kate said, in a failing voice, 'provided you help—help Maurice. I thought it was Maurice. I thought—'

Her voice trailed off.

'She'll be all right in eight or nine hours,' Kennedy said, and edged along the gap towards her; there seemed real concern in his expression. 'That's my little contribution. It's as well she had those tablets, she probably didn't feel half as scared as she would have done otherwise.' He drew the sheets and

81

blankets up about her neck, punched the pillows into position, and stood looking down at her.

Rollison edged along, spotted the knife, picked it up and went into the big room. As he did so, he heard a faint sound outside, and felt quite sure that this was his man, Jolly. He kept to one side and peered on to the landing, for safety's sake. It was Jolly, who was slightly below medium height, in his early sixties, rather pale-faced, and with a bag of skin under his jowl which suggested that he had once been very fat but had lost weight suddenly. His large brown eyes often held a doleful or a puzzled look, but just now he was obviously very wary. He wore a dark grey top coat and a white silk scarf.

'All right, Jolly,' Rollison said. 'We've got some work for you, and we want to get off before Ebbutt's boys arrive. Is that chap all right downstairs?'

Jolly stared at him.

'What chap, sir?' he inquired.

* * * *

'It's absolutely unbelievable,' Kennedy declared harshly. 'I could have sworn I'd put him out for at least twenty minutes! He *couldn't* have gone off on his own.'

'More likely you missed the vital spot,' Rollison said, 'and as he knew you were here he didn't like the odds, so he cut and ran for it. There's just a possibility—' he hesitated, frowning, while Kennedy stared in vexation.

Jolly was washing the cut at Rollison's knee. He had found gauze, a salve and plenty of adhesive plaster, and would do an excellent first aid job.

'What possibility?' demanded Kennedy.

'He could have telephoned for help,' Rollison answered. 'It isn't likely, but we'd better be sure. Jolly, get that done as soon as you can, then go downstairs and wait for Ebbutt's boys. You'll recognise them, but Dr Kennedy won't. Leave two of them downstairs, and bring any more who come along up here with you. If anyone you don't recognise comes, give me a shout.'

'Very well, sir,' Jolly said, and as he

went out, Kennedy's face began to pucker into a grin. Kennedy was never likely to be in a gloomy mood for long, although he still sounded lugubrious when he said:

'The gent's gentleman to the nth degree. How long did it take you to train him?'

'Sometimes I think he trained me,' Rollison answered briskly. 'Mike, we haven't a lot of time to waste. We'll wait until these friends arrive—you know Ebbutt's gymnasium in Whitechapel, don't you?'

'I also know Ebbutt's men would sell their souls for a certain Mr Ar,' answered Kennedy. 'The Torf's a proper Torf to those boyos. And then?'

'Tell Jolly everything we want the police to know, and have him call them,' Rollison went on. 'We'll go and see your contacts at the airport, and find out what we can about the business this evening.'

'Don't mind playing hide and seek with the coppers, I'd much rather you handle this job,' Kennedy said. 'But do we need to go to the airport now? Can't you make Flat Nose tell you all that you need to know? Obviously he's one of the paid staff, surely he must know a lot.'

'We'd be wiser to hand him over to the police,' Rollison said. 'They may know him, and if he hasn't a record, he can start one now. If they think I've handed them a prisoner on a plate they will believe me when I say that I'm co-operating in every possible way!'

Kennedy began to smile.

'And aren't you?'

'I don't understand this job yet,' answered Rollison, with the quizzical expression which would have told Jolly that he was genuinely puzzled indeed. 'I think there's a lot I might be able to find out quicker than the police. This chap is likely to pretend that he's more badly hurt than he is. I wouldn't expect him to start talking for a long time. But there was a "sister", so called, with him at the airport. Now if we could find her—and if we could find out from anything in his pockets where she lives, we might make some progress.'

'You don't improve at all,' remarked Kennedy, drily. 'But I'm game.' He put a hand on Rollison's arm. 'Rolly, I want you to believe one thing: that girl matters to me. You can laugh your head off because I'm such an impressionable clot, but it remains a fact. Count on me to do anything humanly possible.'

'Thanks,' said Rollison.

Then Jolly came upstairs again, to report that William Ebbutt of Whitechapel had sent two men as an advance party. These were downstairs on duty, and others would soon follow. Jolly listened intently to his instructions, did not ask for any of them to be repeated, and when Rollison had finished, said in a voice in which confidence and deference were nicely balanced:

'Very well, sir. The police may know everything, including the fact that there was a young woman—this man's "sister" according to his own statement —who presumably went off with the Alsatian. But they don't know that you have taken the wallet and some letters out of the pockets of the man who escaped. As no one else has appeared, it is hardly likely that he went or sent for assistance, is it, sir?'

'It doesn't look like it,' Rollison

agreed, 'but you can assume the worst until the police take over.'

'I will indeed,' said Jolly.

Obviously he amused Kennedy; as obviously as two lean, middle-aged, tough-looking men who were downstairs by the open front door intrigued him. Each of these touched his forehead to Rollison, each called him Mr Ar, each showed a curious blend of familiarity and obsequiousness which made it even more obvious that Rollison was not regarded like a normal human being. No one else was in the street when they reached the corner and the Rolls-Bentley.

'In you get,' said Rollison, and when they were seated and the doors were closed, he switched on the engine; it hardly made a sound. 'I wonder how long that little shindig took us,' he said musingly. 'Not much more than an hour.'

'So that'll make us an hour late at the airport,' Kennedy observed, and stretched back in his seat, stifled a yawn, and said: 'No one deserves luxury like this, least of all you. We struggling young medicos with our future to make ought to be given one with our first fully satisfied National Health patient. Then we would really do a job. You can let her rip on the Great West Road and out towards the airport,' he went on. 'Is it true that she'll go from a standing start to a hundred and ten miles an hour in less than thirty seconds?'

'Yes,' answered Rollison. ''But not tonight.'

'Let me drive.'

'Not tonight,' repeated Rollison. 'What makes you think we're going to the airport?'

After a moment's pause, Kennedy said blankly: 'Eh?'

'That's the last place I'd go, for the police will be there almost as soon as we would,' reasoned Rollison. 'I said we were going there because Flat Nose was coming round, and he undoubtedly heard it. If Jolly doesn't tell the police, Flat Nose will.'

'Then where the heck *are* we going?'

'We have some addresses,' Rollison said, touching his breast pocket, 'and at any of them we might find this so-called sister and the Alsatian. As you've had RAF training,' Rollison added airily, 'you can take care of the dog.'

CHAPTER 7

Sister?

'Toff,' said Mike Kennedy, after he had been silent for at least thirty seconds, which for him was a long time, 'I would like you to know that for the first time I believe you are as good as your reputation.'

'Or as bad.'

'Good. Did you have to fool Jolly, too?'

'I didn't fool Jolly.'

'Oh,' said Kennedy, humbly. 'It is my night for being the man without a mind. How I let that chap go I'll never—'

'Forget it.'

'I prefer to hate myself.' They were silent for a few minutes, and Rollison turned the car towards the West End. 'May I inquire where we are going? If you prefer just to use me as a door mat, I shall quite understand.'

'There were those addresses,' Rollison repeated, and slid some papers out of his pocket. 'I checked—two are in north-west London, the nearest near Regent's Park, the other out at Hendon. The third address is somewhere near Watford.' As he handed all the papers to Kennedy he went on: 'I didn't have a chance to study them closely—what's the full address of the first one?' He leaned forward, and switched on a panel light, as if for map-reading. 'Can you see?'

'Only my mind is closed.' There was a pause. 'The first address is a Mr Jeremiah Whittaker at 40, Park View, St. John's Wood. That the first port of call?'

'Yes.'

'Are we going to commit burglary?'

'Any objection?'

'I don't know whether you realise just how tough and clever these Alsatians can be,' Kennedy said, uneasily. 'I'm not worried about getting a bite, but it might not be possible to stop the brute from barking. Er—unless—'

'Unless what?'

'Forearmed is better than fore-warned,' said Kennedy, earnestly, and gave Rollison the impression that he was thinking very fast. 'As I'm in this up to the neck, I may as well let the waters of wickedness lap over my head. I could nip back to my surgery, get a hypo and some dope. I could then make cooing sounds, and—'

Rollison was already slowing down, to turn round; it took only ten minutes to make the return trip to Kennedy's surgery.

'Thanks,' said Kennedy, humbly. 'I felt that I must do something to make amends.' As they drove off again, he went on: 'Did you know that you're the most uncommunicative chap when you want to be? No one could say you haven't talked, but how much have you really said? I mean,' went on Kennedy, earnestly, 'what do you think about it all? What do you think happened to Kate's Maurice?'

'That's anyone's guess,' Rollison observed drily.

'I'd prefer your guess to anyone else's fact.'

'I shouldn't, if I were you,' advised
Rollison. 'I once guessed that a gun was
empty, and spent three months in
hospital as a result. There isn't any need
to guess, anyhow. One of two things
happened to Maurice Holmes—either he
was lured or spirited away against his
will, or he went off of his own free will.'

'Damn it, you can't think he was
shanghaied in front of a hundred
customers at the airport!'

'He might have been blackmailed, or
put under some pressure to do exactly
what he was told,' Rollison reasoned,
'and it may have been essential to stop
Kate from seeing him—or him from
seeing Kate. That's the heart of the
problem, and don't tell me that I wallow
in clichés.'

'You can utter a cliché a minute and it
won't make any difference to me,' said
Kennedy. 'I'm completely sold on you,
Toff. Any preference for one theory or
the other? Was he stopped from seeing
Kate, or was Kate stopped from seeing
him?'

'Kate was stopped from seeing him.'

'What makes you think so?'

'Because she was attacked again so soon afterwards,' reasoned Rollison, and went on more expansively than usual, for it was not like him to explain his reasoning except to Jolly or to the police: 'That's what made me so anxious about her. If one attempt was made to prevent her from seeing Holmes, would there be others? If there were others, how many, and would any be permanent?'

'I see,' said Kennedy, very quietly. 'Plain as the nose on my ugly dial when I have it explained to me as precisely as that. So, someone wants to prevent her from seeing Maurice Holmes again. Do you think that's right?'

'It's a fairly safe bet, but it might not be the only reason for the attack on her.'

'Why should anyone want to prevent her from seeing him?' asked Kennedy. 'I mean, what logical reason could there be?' When Rollison did not answer, he went on: 'It doesn't make any sense to me. After all, everyone knows he arrived. He's got to see his boss at Malling Motors and his business associates fairly soon. Why should anyone set out just to stop *her* from seeing him?'

Rollison said, heavily: 'Ah.'

'Ah what?'

'Just ah,' repeated Rollison, and glanced at his companion. He had been driving very steadily through the almost deserted streets, and was now moving fairly fast along Baker Street, heading for Regent's Park. Some of the few pedestrians turned to stare at the car as it passed.

Kennedy insisted: 'You mean, there might be attempts to stop *others* from seeing him?'

'There could be.'

'*Others* are in danger?' As always when he was bewildered, Kennedy's voice rose.

'Could be,' agreed Rollison. 'Or Holmes could simply be kept away from the others. Kate was the only person likely to meet him at the airport, and so the only one bound to see him as he came through that Customs Bay. We'll find out if he makes contact with Malling Motors in the morning.'

'A thousand to one he won't,' guessed Kennedy.

'You're probably right,' said Rollison. 'Supposing we stop trying to see the end of this job until we can really understand the beginning? Park View is the second or third on the left up here, I believe.'

He swung the car off the main road, drove along a dark and winding road for two or three minutes, passing two turnings to the right; the left side was just the intense darkness of Regent's Park. The headlamps shone on lamp posts, the lights of which had been switched off, reflected from the windows of tall houses, then on to a white gate with a number written clearly on it: 40, Park View.

'So it's on a corner,' he mused, 'and it stands in grounds on its own. We'll park a hundred yards along, and walk back. How do you feel?'

'About the same as I always do when I think I might make a meal for an Alsatian,' Kennedy answered. 'I'll be all right, Rolly. I don't pretend that I'm not a bit jumpy, but I won't let the side down.'

Rollison saw him smile.

The left the car parked with its sidelights on, and walked briskly back towards the corner house. The roof showed up square and black against a dark grey sky; only here and there were stars visible. Now and again a gust of wind swept from behind them with unexpected force, and trees set up a great rustling. Somewhere an iron gate clanged, nearer them a wooden gate kept creaking. The white posts of Number 40 showed up clearly. There were two gates after all, one on Park View, one on a side street. Their feet crunched on thick gravel. No light was on anywhere, except from a glow in the sky, and the house itself seemed to be in complete darkness.

'My chief worry has four legs, a tail and a lot of teeth,' Kennedy remarked *sotto voce*. 'Which way do you propose to break in?'

'*I* don't propose to break in,' said Rollison.

'*What's* that?' As they approached the front porch, which also seemed to be painted white, Kennedy turned a startled face towards Rollison. 'I thought that was where you had the advantage over the coppers! They have to get a search warrant and knock at the door, you find the nearest open window and snoop without permission.'

'I propose to knock, this time,' Rollison said. 'You do the breaking in.'

'Now listen, Rolly—' Kennedy began, but did not finish.

They stepped on to the porch.

Rollison was smiling to himself as he went on: 'You stay out of sight, and we'll see what happens. That window of the room immediately above the porch is open, and if I seem to need help, you nip up there is necessary. I'll try to leave the front door on the latch, and that may be the easier way for you to get in.'

'I don't know that I like this much,' said Kennedy, ruefully. 'Why don't I knock at the door for the official reception, and you be the furtive marauder?'

'Because if they see you they'll suspect that I'm probably round the corner, but if they see me they'll probably assume that I've been fool enough to come alone.' Rollison put his finger on the bell push and kept it there for what seemed a very long time. 'Also, my knee is prejudiced against too much action.' There was no sound of ringing; the only sound was a car which swept along Park View, headlights shining on trees and bushes and telegraph poles, and making black windows look like gargoyles' eyes. It scorched round a corner and gradually the sound faded. 'It wouldn't surprise me too much if the place is empty,' Rollison added.

'Why the heck should it be?'

Rollison said patiently: 'Because of the man who got away. He could have telephoned. If he did he would report that he had lost his wallet and so I had this address, and might hand it over to the police. If there was anything to worry about here—such as Maurice Holmes, for instance—they would want to get away quickly.'

'I get it,' said Kennedy, humbly. 'Ask Jolly to give me a few elementary lessons in How The Toff Reasons And Why He Does It So Quickly.'

'Mick,' said Rollison, and stabbed the bell push again.

'Yes?'

'Just pause to think.'

'Ah,' said Kennedy, still ruefully. 'If I'm not dealing with coughs and colds and *rigor mortis,* I never give myself time to think.' He paused, and then added: 'It does rather seem to me as if there's no response, doesn't it? Shall we try the back door?'

'I'll try knocking,' said Rollison.

He gave a sharp rat-tat-tat on the brass knocker, and the banging seemed to reverberate about the porch and the grounds, and then to fade away into silence. No sound came from the house.

'I'll go and see what the situation is at the back,' said Rollison. 'You wait here until the copper comes. When he wants to know what you're doing here and why you're making so much noise on the knocker, say you're extremely sorry, but you're staying here for the night. With luck,' added Rollison, 'I'll open the front door to you while he's asking questions.'

'But how do you know—' began Kennedy.

'The London copper never misses anything,' declared Rollison, straight-faced.

He slid out of the porch and towards the corner of the house, and then disappeared. He peered up at all the windows of the house, at the back and at both sides, a careful reconnaissance which showed no lights, no sound, and only two open windows. It took him seven or eight minutes. Then, nearing the front of the house, he thought that he heard the crunch of bicycle wheels on the gravel of the road. He reached the back of the house again, and looked about him. A large garage stood some way back, and appeared to be built against a high wall which made one of the walls of the garage. There was a lawn surrounded by bushes, and outside the house itself a patch of concrete with one or two small sheds built out from the house. The back door was covered by a little roof, but there was no porch. The top of the window near this door was open a few inches, which seemed to imply that the householder had no special fear of burglary.

Rollison pulled on a pair of thin cotton gloves, then tried the handle of the back door, and found the door locked. He took out the knife which had some remarkable blades, fiddled for a few seconds, and heard the lock click back. When he pushed, the door yielded, so it wasn't bolted. He stepped inside, and the door creaked. He was on the alert for the slightest hint that there might be a dog waiting for him; it would not be the first time he had been pounced on, and the memory of one particular case concerning dogs always filled him with a sense of horror.

He *smelt* a doggy kind of odour, the curious mustiness and the smell of dog food which permeated this room, but he heard and saw nothing. He switched on the light, and looked about a scullery with a large old-fashioned sink and, in one corner, a large old-fashioned brick copper. By the sink was a huge, brown earthenware dish, marked *Mine*. In it were scraps of a mushy looking meal and some dog biscuits. By it was a white vegetable dish which had a big crack in it, half-filled with water. He stepped through this room into the kitchen beyond. This had been modernised and was very bright and shiny—and in one corner was a huge dog basket. There was no sound in here.

He stepped through a doorway, which was ajar, and as he did so heard a murmur of voices; he felt quite sure that these came from the porch. He smothered a grin at Kennedy's likely reaction to that, and heard Kennedy protest:

'I can't exactly *help* being locked out, can I?'

Rollison stepped slowly forward. The light from behind him would shine on the glass panels of the door, and both Kennedy and the policeman would have noticed it by now. He put his hat on the newel post of the bannisters, stepped past an open doorway, confident that once he opened the door it would satisfy the policeman.

Then he glanced through the open doorway.

'...there's a light!' exclaimed Kennedy. 'Someone's awake!'

Rollison heard him, and yet the words seemed to have lost their significance; everything lost its significance because of the sight in front of him. Just inside that doorway, lying on a couch which stood cornerwise across a small room, lay a girl.

He could not see her face.

He could see the way her head drooped over the side of the couch, hair falling down in an odd way, and he could see the utter stillness of the body—as well as the stocking, or what looked like a stocking, embedded in her neck.

CHAPTER 8

Poor Kid

Rollison stood absolutely still. There was silence on the porch, too, as if the men could not understand why he did not come forward. The sight of the girl's fair hair hanging down had a horrid fascination, and for a few seconds he could not make himself move away. At last he stretched forward, pulled the door to cautiously, and went to the front door. He knew exactly what he would have to do and how he wanted to do it, but it wouldn't be easy to behave as if nothing had happened.

'I tell you I'm going to ring and knock again,' Mike said, as if exasperated beyond all patience.

'I think I can hear someone coming, sir,' the policeman said, placatingly.

Rollison glanced at the top and bottom

of the door. No bolts were shot home, all
he had to do was twist the handle and
pull. His fingers were very cold and his
arm seemed stiff when he did so, but as
the door opened and he stood back, he
gave a smile which no one would think
was strained, stifled a yawn, and said:

'Dammit, Mike, did you have to wake
the street?'

'I had to wake *you.*'

'And you did.' Rollison glanced at the
policeman, and stifled another yawn.
'Don't say you were going to get the
police to let you in!'

'As a matter of fact, the gentleman
was making so much noise that I thought
I had better come and make sure that he
was not the worse for alcohol,' said the
policeman, solemnly. He was a middle-
aged man, tall and thin, and he seemed to
be fully satisfied. 'Is everything all right,
sir?'

'Perfectly all right. This gentleman is
staying with me for a few days. He *did*
have a key.'

'Lost it,' declared Mike, sadly. Then
he brightened. 'But one shouldn't look a
gift bed-sitter in the broken window,

106

should one? Thanks a lot, officer.' He stepped inside, as Rollison drew back.

'That's all right, sir. Goodnight.'

'...night,' Rollison echoed.

He watched the policeman trudge towards his bicycle, which was leaning against a bush at one side of the drive, and then closed the door. The moment the policeman was cut off from sight, Rollison saw a mind picture of that girl on the couch. Kennedy was beaming and rubbing his hands together, and presumably he had no reason to suspect that anything was wrong.

'I'm beginning to tumble to the Toff's tactics,' he said. 'Never hit the old bod in the same place twice? I can imagine how you make the Yard johnnies feel as if they're running round in hula hoops sometimes. Er—'

He broke off.

'Rolly,' he said, in a different tone of voice, 'what's worrying you? Everything's all right, isn't it?'

'No,' answered Rollison, now in complete control of himself.

He had seen many worse sights, and would again; it had been the suddenness and the unexpectedness of what he had seen here which had unnerved him. Now, he wanted to get Mike Kennedy's reaction the moment Mike saw the same thing without getting any serious warning.

'What's up?' Mike demanded.

'The place is empty, and I don't like it,' Rollison said. 'Just check in that room, will you?' He pointed to the door which he had pulled to, and Kennedy pushed it open with his right hand, stepped inside, switched on the light—and stopped short. Rollison saw his change of expression, the way in which his jaw worked, as if he clenched his teeth. In a strange way, Mike Kennedy seemed to age ten years in ten seconds.

He turned to stare at Rollison.

'No wonder you looked as if someone had kicked you in the guts,' he said, bleakly. 'But why spring this on me?' When Rollison didn't answer, he went forward, bent down on one knee, and gently raised the girl's head and shoulders. Her mouth was slack, her eyes half-closed. He shifted her position a little, and felt for her pulse. Rollison touched the back of her neck, and made sure that a twisted stocking was the murder weapon; he did not doubt for a second that the girl was dead.

Mike Kennedy straightened up.

'She's a gonner,' he announced.

Rollison nodded.

'Think she was this "sister"?'

'I think she must have known a lot which we weren't to find out from her,' Rollison said, harshly. 'I think—' he broke off.

'If we'd come half an hour sooner, we might have saved her,' Kennedy said savagely.

'If we'd come half an hour sooner, Kate Lowson might be dead, instead of this woman,' Rollison said, and threw his shoulders back as if this were a physical burden which he could shift if he tried hard enough. 'Mike, I want to look through this place quickly, just in case we can pick up some odds and ends we might be able to use but the police couldn't.'

Kennedy stared at him.

'Isn't it time you stopped this play-acting, and for the police to take over?

This is murder, or didn't you know that?'

Rollison said: 'There's a telephone in that corner, Mike. If you want the police here inside two minutes, dial 999. I'm going to look round. I shouldn't move that body—the police don't like it when bodies are moved.' He glanced about the room, saw nothing that interested him, for this looked like a small morning-and-sewing room, and went out. He put on all the lights as he went about the house. There were three large rooms downstairs, including a billiards room. He searched a sideboard, a writing bureau and two tables, but found nothing which he thought would be of real interest. He was looking for those missing letters and for a pile of money which might have been stolen recently.

He went upstairs.

None of the beds had been slept in, but two or three dressing-tables had obviously been emptied in a hurry. Only one room had any women's clothes. He went in a small room, and stopped short. In the corner was a safe, its door open and the shelves empty except for a few odds and ends which he felt sure would not be of any help to him. This was a little office, and the drawers of the only desk and of a green steel filing cabinet were also open. He glanced in these. There was plenty that the police would want to look at, but obviously anything likely to be important had been taken away in the panic rush from this house.

The explanation of this seemed so obvious that he began to wonder if it could be the true one; that the man who had escaped had telephoned a message, and that this girl had been killed as a result of it.

He went up to the third and last floor, and found that the rooms were empty and dusty, except one which was filled with old furniture, pieces of bedding, some empty suitcases, an old wardrobe trunk festooned with labels, and a tailor's dummy. He went downstairs. He found Kennedy in the room with the dead girl. Kennedy was looking at him bleakly.

'Are you going to send for the police now?'

Rollison said: 'Mike, what's got

111

into you?'

'You know damned well what's got into me.'

'Spell it out for me.'

'You don't need anything spelt out,' said Kennedy harshly. 'I wondered what you looked at me like that for when we'd got rid of the copper. The man who got away telephoned here, and as a result this poor kid was strangled. That makes it my fault. I am a doctor. I am also something of a physical culture expert. You know that. The man I was supposed to have knocked out got up and walked away— so this *is* my fault. If it is, why? Because I'm a bloody, incompetent fool, or because I had a reason for letting the man escape?'

Kennedy paused; and when he went on, each word was like the lash of a whip:

'Well? Is that Machiavellian enough for the great Toff?'

Rollison said, slowly: 'Yes, it's about right, Mike, and I'd be a fool if I didn't begin to wonder why you came for me, and what really happened with the man who got away. If the police are told that you're involved, they'll think the same way as I do. They'll probably hold you, at least for questioning. They'll make a good job of it, too, and the newspapers will soon find out. There'll be little or no chance of you doing anything else on this job, and you might find yourself on a charge.'

Kennedy asked, harshly: 'A charge of what?'

'Strangling this girl, for instance.'

'Don't be a fool. You were with me.'

'Not all the time,' Rollison said, quietly. 'You were on your own for about ten minutes. The police don't know that, but they won't necessarily believe me if I lie. They make a habit of doubting me whenever they think I'm trying to cover up for someone else. If we send for the police right away, you will have put yourself out of my control. If we leave and let them discover this for themselves, or even telephone a message to make them come here, you and I can work out our problem.'

Mike Kennedy said: 'What good will that do? If you think I let the fellow go deliberately, and think I might have killed that girl—'

'Mike,' said Rollison, and something in the tone of his voice suggested that he was at the end of his patience, 'you don't have to do what I suggest. You can do whatever you think best. But if you send for the police now, you'll be proving just one thing. You'll be proving that you don't want me and you don't want yourself to go on searching for the murderer. You'll be putting a spanner into our works. Is that what you want?'

'Would you mind telling me how I can make you believe that all I know about this business is what I've told you?'

'Time,' answered Rollison.

He glanced at the girl. Had there been the faintest chance that anyone could help, he would have called the Yard the moment he had found her. Now he believed that there was a greater chance of avenging her if he spent some time here before the police. He did not try to force Kennedy's hand any more, and was not really surprised when Kennedy said:

'Oh, you'd better have it your own way.'

'Good,' said Rollison, briskly. 'Now,

there's only one place in this house we haven't visited yet—that's the cellar. Let's go and have a look round.' He moved towards the door which he had noticed under the stairs; in Victorian houses of this kind the cellar was often approached in that way. He turned the handle, careful to use a glove so that he did not leave any prints, and the door opened without any trouble.

'Look out for that so-and-so dog,' Kennedy muttered.

Rollison stood with the door open an inch or two, listening; and he was quite sure that if a dog had been breathing close to the door, he would have heard it. So he shone a torch about the little landing at the top of the stone steps, found the electric switch, and pressed it down. Bright light flooded the top and the foot of the stairs. The stairs were of wood, they looked freshly scrubbed, and they had a hollow kind of echo as the two men walked down. Kennedy gave the impression that he was very much on edge. Rollison limped ahead, and reached the foot of the stairs. There was a little passage, with a closed door to the right and an open one straight in front. He smelt oil, and guessed that an oil-fired central heating plant was in the smaller part of the cellar.

He pushed open the closed door, groped for a light, and pressed it down.

On the floor lay a great Alsatian—stretched out stiffly, as obviously dead as the girl had been.

CHAPTER 9

Detective Inspector Meer

After a moment of silence, Kennedy said explosively: 'So I didn't need my dope.' Rollison didn't answer, but looked about the cellar. It was more orderly and much cleaner than most, and was used for storing food and wine—along one wall there were at least twenty wine bins, several of them practically full, and only in them had cobwebs been allowed to gather. Empty boxes were stacked along one side. There were at least two hundred empty wine bottles all standing on shelves and on the floor, like gleaming sentries.

On a wooden Windsor chair in front of an old deal topped table was a snap-brimmed trilby hat. On the table was an open brief-case. By the brief-case were several manilla folders, two of them open, the others closed. The intials on the case did not show up clearly until Rollison moved forward a yard. Then he saw: *M.K.H.*

Kennedy edged towards him.

'No one said his middle name began with K,' he muttered, 'but it looks as if it did. Kenneth, Kevin, Keith?' He stepped over the body of the dog, and said: 'To do that justice we really want to bring Van Gogh back to life, no one else ever made a chair mean anything. If only that seat could speak.' The joke fell flat. 'Why bring him down here?' Before Rollison had a chance to answer, he went on: 'At least we haven't found his body.'

'Yet,' said Rollison drily. He went to the folders and fingered them so that he could see the papers inside; there were rows upon rows of columns, which looked like stock lists of spare motor car parts, and hundreds upon hundreds of carbon copies of letters; these seemed to be all the files which Holmes had had with him. The brief-case contained a pair of glasses, two ball-point pens, a small ruler, a pen-knife and some rubber bands, as well as several thick scrap pads.

Most of the letters were addressed to a *James Wedlake, Esq., Malling Motors Sales Division, London, W.I.*

'Quite a boy for work,' Kennedy remarked.

'I wonder if they stole his love letters, too,' said Rollison.

'Eh? Why should they?'

'Don't take me too literally, Mike. We can be sure that Holmes was brought down here, and it rather looks as if he was questioned while tied to the chair.'

'If they didn't kill him, then obviously he's more valuable to them alive than dead,' observed Kennedy sagely, and then appeared to realise the inanity of this remark and went on hurriedly: 'What I mean is, they want him alive but they'd gladly kill Kate.'

'Yes,' said Rollison. 'Notice anything else?'

Kennedy hesitated, looked round, sniffed, and shook his head.

'The smell of oil, that's all.'

'The people who own this house, or at least who live in it, believe in eating well,' Rollison pointed out. 'Only true gourmets would worry about such a variety of wine and brandy as this.' He went to a bin, picked up a small bottle and studied it almost reverently: 'Napoleon,' he said, and put the bottle back. Then he saw a torn label tied to a small crate, bent down, and read: *Jeremiah W*— The rest of the name was torn off.

'Yet they were so scared that they got out at a moment's notice.'

'If they've been here a long time, we should be able to trace 'em pretty quickly,' Rollison said, and frowned. 'I don't know what it is, but there's a pretty little trick being played here. This is a man's cellar, probably an old man's cellar. Few white wines, few light wines —brandies and liqueurs, no champagne to speak of. Hmm. Mike,' Rollison went on, more quickly, 'did Kate Lowson tell you the name of Holmes's uncle—the one you said she said had died?'

'Well, no, but—she said something about a deceased Uncle Jerry.'

'An old man's cellar, a heap of Victorian junk upstairs, a whole floor not lived in, a Jeremiah W—it could shape up,' Rollison went on, almost as if he were speaking to himself. 'It's worth—'

He broke off.

The sound of a car came clearly, and he glanced up at the far corner of the ceiling, where there was a ventilation grille; undoubtedly the sound was travelling through that. The car noises became much louder. Kennedy began to fidget, and Rollison raised a hand. Then, there was the sound of gears being changed. The engine roared, and seemed to be almost on top of them. Suddenly, the car stopped. There was a slight squealing noise, and a moment later the engine was switched off. Immediately, that of another car a little further away could be heard. Doors opened, and footsteps sounded.

'What the devil's all this about,' demanded Kennedy.

'The police haven't lost much time,' Rollison said, mildly. 'Now we have to decide whether to let them find us, or try to get away.'

After a pause, Kennedy said thinly: 'Personally, I'm in favour of getting away. I'd prefer not to be found on the premises with a woman who's been strangled, especially as I can't rely on you to give me full supporting evidence. But how do we go?'

As he finished, there was the sound of a bell ringing; a moment later, the banging of the front door knocker.

'And I wonder what brought them here,' he said. 'Er—Rolly, do you really think we've got a chance of getting away?'

Rollison said, thoughtfully: 'I haven't, as I can't run, but I think you have if you'll do it my way.' He went upstairs to the telephone, and dialled 999, very deliberately.

* * * *

'Thanks,' said Mike Kennedy, and he sounded almost humble. 'I'll do the same for you one day. 'Er—how?'

'There are two carloads of policemen,' Rollison said. 'Say eight men—ten at the most, but ten's not likely. I'll go and let them in.' He broke off, and said into the telephone: 'Please tell the police to come at once to Number 40, Park View, Regent's Park.' He replaced the receiver, and went on: 'As soon as they realise that there's a corpse, these chaps will send to the Yard by radio telephone, and they'll want to gawp at the body. Even policemen always do. You take your chance and slip out the front way. Don't run, don't do anything to attract attention —just slip through the garden, climb over the wall and get next door, and then find your way home. Right?'

'It *sounds* easy,' Kennedy said dubiously.

'You can make it easy,' Rollison assured him confidently. He heard the banging again and moved slowly towards the doors. 'No need to let them start breaking the door down.' He limped up the stairs as fast as he could, with Kennedy just behind him. As they entered the passage, there was another thunderous knocking at the front door.

'Coming!' called Rollison.

He went ahead, and hid even Kennedy's shadow from sight of anyone who might be peering through the letter box. He gave Kennedy time to go into the front room, then opened the door. He wasn't surprised to see three heavily-built men on the porch in a solid phalanx, as if they meant to make sure that he could not rush them and so escape. Hovering on the perimeter behind them was a fourth man. Two cars were drawn up, one on either side.

'I am a police officer,' the first man announced, Rollison vaguely recognised him, and wondered how much longer it would be before he was recognised in turn. 'Are you Mr Maurice Holmes?'

'No,' answered Rollison, and concealed his surprise at that question. 'Should I be?' He heard a click, and a beam of light shot out from the other's torch, shining brightly on to his face and making him screw up his eyes against the glare. There was a moment's pause, and then one of the others exclaimed:

'It's that man Rollison!'

'That's right,' said Rollison, 'and if you wouldn't mind switching off the floodlight I might be able to see if you really are a copper or whether you're trying to pull a fast one.' The light was switched off at once, and he peered at the man who had spoken and who was now taking a card out of his pocket. 'All right,' he went on briskly, 'you're Detecive Inspector Meer, aren't you? R.P. Division. And you couldn't be more welcome. You've a murder case on your hands. I've just dialled 999.'

One man exclaimed: 'Murder?' No one else spoke. Rollison had often noticed the effect that the realisation of murder had, even on policemen who were hardened to it. He stood aside as Meer, a heavily-built man wearing an unexpectedly small hat which looked a little ridiculous, stepped in. The others followed—except the man on the perimeter. Meer reached the little room, took one look, and then turned round and barked orders.

'Bert, call the Yard, tell them what's happened, get someone off from Prints p.d.q. Tell Wilson outside to telephone the Old Man. Forbes—go through to the back, let the chaps there in, and start looking round. Make a thorough job of it. The body's still warm so she hasn't been dead long. Mr Rollison, wait here, please.'

As a piece of adminstrative organisation it was very impressive, and it sent everyone who had come with Meer out of the room except a sergeant with a notebook. Meer bent down on one knee and did exactly what Kennedy had done to the girl. Rollison stood in the doorway, watching, expecting to hear an outcry at any moment, but after three or four minutes he felt quite sure that Kennedy had got safely away.

Kennedy was a remarkable young man in a lot of ways, and knew how to keep his head.

Meer turned to Rollison.

'Now if you'll tell us what you are doing here, I'll be glad, sir. Don't talk too quickly, please, Sergeant Dickson will want to take everything you say down in shorthand. First of all, why did you come here?'

Rollison grinned.

'If you knew how badly I want to know what brought you, you wouldn't have started off like that!'

Meer made no attempt to smile, and his rugged face looked forbidding and dull.

'Just make your statement, sir, please,' he insisted.

'All right,' said Rollison obligingly.

'But don't forget my first comment, will you? That I had just dialled 999.'

'That's as may be,' said Detective Inspector Meer.

He was not going to be easy, and he would probably be even more difficult when the local police arrived and reported that Rollison had admitted another man, who was supposed to be staying on the premises. The simple thing would be to say that Kennedy had come with a message, and that he had claimed to be staying here so as to reassure the policeman. Meer might not like it, but it would be hard to disprove.

Meer was a minor problem. It was difficult to concentrate on him, even enough to mitigate his nuisance value. The startling facts concerned the disappearance of Holmes from the aircraft, the indications that he had been brought here, the fact that the girl and the dog had been killed here, and that a man with a flattened nose had tried to kill Kate Lowson at her flat. Add this to Meer's question: "Are you Mr Maurice Holmes?" and it turned the problem upside down—for it made it fairly evident that Meer expected to find Holmes as a resident here. Yet he had been abroad, and Kate Lowson had booked a hotel for him.

'One of the things I should have asked,' Rollison said musingly, and saw Meer glance up sharply. He hadn't started to make his statement yet, and the sergeant with Meer was sharpening his pencil.

'What's that?'

'Nothing. Did you expect to find Holmes here?'

'It wouldn't be surprising to find a man in his own house, would it?'

So Meer, in being truculent, was being helpful. Rollison was humble.

'No,' he admitted. 'Foolish of me. But—er—he didn't live here before his uncle died, had he?'

'He's lived here for years,' retorted Meer. 'I thought you were the man who was supposed to know everything.'

'Lord, no,' said Rollison. 'I'm no policeman!' He saw the sergeant start, then smother a grin; saw Meer jerk his head up, and wondered whether he had annoyed the man too much. It was a silly crack with one who had already proven himself touchy. Then to his surprise and relief, Meer broke out with a guffaw of laughter.

'All right, Mr Rollison, you've had your little joke,' he said. 'Now how about getting that statement down so that I can let you go and get the mystery solved for us? No use having the Toff stalling around at our slow pace, is it?' He burst out with laughter at this sally, and as the sergeant poised his pencil, he went on: 'Just between you and me, Mr Rollison, can you give us any angle that might save us time? Why did you come here, for instance?

'Looking for Holmes.'

'Why, since you didn't know he lived here?' asked Meer, ingenuously.

Rollison found himself warming to the man; here was an astute detective who knew exactly what he was doing.

'Inspector,' Rollison said, 'I went to see his girl friend. She was attacked. I caught her assailant, checked some addresses in his pocket—and here I am. Believe it or not, I didn't first find out where Holmes was likely to be. He's been here, though; and the dog which tripped Miss Lowson up at the airport is down in the cellar, dead of poisoning.'

'Ah,' said Meer, and rubbed his chin. 'The murderer and the dog poisoner couldn't have been that gentleman whom you let in earlier, could it? Dr Kennedy, I mean.'

CHAPTER 10

Trust?

'Meer,' said Rollison, and this time he felt as well as sounded humble, 'you are a far better man than I. Tonight.'

Meer's big teeth looked very white as he grinned, obviously with real satisfaction.

'I wouldn't say that, Mr Rollison, even we flatfoots have to have some breaks. After Dr Kennedy's questions about the missing passengers, the Airport Police told the Yard what had happened this evening, and so we were pretty well briefed. When your man Jolly called the Chelsea Division, naturally Division called us.'

'Why naturally?' inquired Rollison.

'Well, sir, old Jeremiah Whittaker was well known in this district—that's Mr Holmes's uncle—the Holmes had rooms here when he was in England. He'd lived here for forty years, Mr Whittaker had, he was quite a lad. If it hadn't been for gout and a bit of arthritis in his right hip he would have been a lot more of a lad. Believe it or not, he couldn't get a house-keeper to stay with him more than a few weeks, the bawdy old—but we mustn't speak ill of the dead.'

'Were you speaking ill of him?' asked Rollison, mildly.

Meer guffawed again.

'Depends how you look at it, I suppose. You'll admit that it was a natural sequence of events. And when we found out from our chap on the beat that you'd been here, and admitted a man who answered Dr Kennedy's description —well, we didn't take long to add things up, did we? One of your dis-advantages, sir, if you don't mind me saying so, is that every policeman in London knows you on sight. Or he ought to!'

Rollison laughed.

'I give up. But the answer to one half of your question is a positive "no" and to the other half a probable "no".'

Meer put his head on one side, contemplatively, and then his eyes lit up, and his memory served him and he said with obvious satisfaction:

'Which is the positive "no", sir? Could Dr Kennedy have poisoned the dog or strangled the young woman?'

'He couldn't have poisoned the dog.'

'Might be as well as if he could have,' said Meer musingly. 'Did he have a real chance to injure the girl?'

'Ten minutes, at most—including getting in and persuading her to let him put the stocking round her neck. Also, he would have had to have a stocking in his pocket or go up to her bedroom and get one—unless there was some washing hanging up in the kitchen, but I don't recollect seeing any.' said Rollison. 'I don't think you'd have much chance of a case against Dr Kennedy.'

'Where is he?'

'On his way home.'

'So you managed to get him away, did you?' asked Meer, and rubbed his block of a chin. 'I daresay you'd have got away, too, if it hadn't been for your injured knee. That's not too bad, is it?'

'It could be worse.'

'Like some more first aid?'

'No, I'll leave it as it is,' said Rollison. He took out cigarettes, offered them, and went on as Meer struck a match: 'What else do you want from me?'

'Taken by and large, sir, I think you've told us the only important thing we want to know,' Meer declared, and stood frowning and drawing heavily on his cigarette, vaguely like an ape learning to smoke. He had very little, brown eyes and very shaggy eyebrows. He went on musingly: 'We know more or less when you arrived, you couldn't have had much time to do anything, you've told us the truth about Kennedy—there's just one thing, sir.'

'What's that?'

'Don't take offence, but would you mind if we had a look through your pockets? I mean, you might have come across something in this house and absent-mindedly tucked it away—just as well that we make sure that you don't take anything which might help us in our inquiries, sir, isn't it?'

Rollison chuckled as deeply as he had

for a long time; deeply enough to forget the sight of the dead girl. He emptied his pockets. Among the things which he brought out was the .32 revolver, taken from the man outside Kate Lawson's place. Meer considered this very thoughtfully, but made no comment. The only papers which interested him were those which Rollison had taken from the two men in Gillivry Street—and as Rollison knew, these were useful only in so far as they gave the names and addresses of the two men. Now, the police knew of the other two addresses which he would have visited if he had drawn a blank here. Meer studied the letters solemnly, and then as solemnly handed them back.

'Nothing of value there, sir. Sure there's nothing you've taken from here?'

'You didn't give me time,' mourned Rollison. 'You wouldn't expect me to want to be caught red-handed, would you?'

'Must be most trying to be handicapped with your knee as it is,' said Meer. 'Is that gun yours?'

'No. It belongs to the man who was concerned in the attack on Miss Lowson.

135

He threatened me with it.'

'Then I'd better have it, sir,' said Meer. 'I don't think I need worry you any more, Mr Rollison. If Dr Kennedy gets in touch with you tonight, I hope you will make quite sure that we know at once. Now—can I let you have a man to drive you back to Gresham Terrace? One of our chaps is a wow of a driver, and when he saw your car round the corner his eyes nearly popped out of his head.'

'Let him drive me,' Rollison said. 'A policeman's eyes popping would be a sight I'd like to see tonight. Thanks, inspector.'

'*My* privilege,' Meer said, and then cocked an ear to sounds outside. The first of the reinforcements were here: ambulance, police-car, or car with the Fingerprint experts; Meer seemed to have a genius for timing, as he went towards the door, calling 'Wilson!' The man who had hovered behind the phalanx in the porch came forward, and exclaimed:

'Would I *mind!*'

Twenty minutes later, turning into the Piccadilly end of Gresham Terrace, that street in the heart of Mayfair where

136

Rollison had lived for over twenty years, Wilson said in tones almost of awe:

'Loveliest job I've ever driven, sir. Any time you want to give this away, you know who'd like it, don't you?'

'I'll remember you,' Rollison said, solemnly. They pulled up outside Number 22. 'Thanks, Wilson. If you ever want to leave the Force and take a chauffeur's job, you won't forget me, will you?'

'Now that's *very* nice of you, sir,' said Wilson warmly, and got out of the car and opened Rollison's door, handed him out, and went on: 'Mind you, I'm not likely to leave the Force, although it's a hell of a bind sometimes. You can never tell when you're going to have an evening off, and the way they pay you, you'd think we were fresh out of Dartmoor. Can you manage to get up the stairs, sir?'

'Yes, thanks,' said Rollison. 'It wouldn't surprise me if my man doesn't come to my rescue, anyhow.'

'That Jolly,' said Wilson, and chuckled. 'He's a proper card.'

The street door of the house opened, and the "proper card" appeared, obviously both anxious and eager. Wilson waited until the door closed, and then turned and walked briskly away. Jolly had a hand at Rollison's elbow as they reached the bottom of the first flight of stairs, and as Rollison listened to the sound of fading footsteps.

He grinned.

'He's gone,' he said, and began to walk up the stairs almost normally. Jolly, a step behind him, looked mildly surprised. Rollison turned and glanced over his shoulder, and said: 'It's nothing like as bad as I want the police to think it is, it might be useful to have them believe I'm *hors de combat* for a few days. Remind me to remember to limp.'

'I'm very glad it's no worse, sir. When I saw you being driven by the other man, I feared that the injury was much less superficial than I had judged when I bandaged it at Miss Lowson's apartment,' Jolly said.

'How is Miss Lowson?'

'Fast asleep, sir. These modern drugs are *quite* remarkable.'

'Quite. How many men are looking after her?'

'The situation is very nearly unprecedented,' said Jolly, and thrust open the door of the top apartment. They stepped into a wide entrance hall, furnished with a suite of modern furniture, with a writing desk, a telephone against one wall, some magazines and newspapers on a small table, and two etchings on the walls. 'Mr Ebbutt's reinforcements arrived, so there are four of his men in all, and the Chelsea police are also making sure that there isn't any danger to the young lady. I—ah—suggested that one of Ebbutt's men, Percy Wrightson, should stay in the flat. So one of the policemen was also detailed to remain there.' Jolly's usually sombre face was positively bright with a smile. 'When I left, Wrightson was on the couch, with his feet up, a bottle of beer beside him, and some comic books—and the Chelsea detective officer was sitting in the kitchen on a very uncomfortable chair. Most amusing, sir!'

Rollison chuckled, and stepped into the larger room, the living-room, of his flat.

Standing with his back to a long wall which seemed to be filled with lethal weapons, was Mike Kennedy.

* * * *

Kennedy did not move as Rollison stepped inside. Jolly stood away from the door, after closing it with hardly a sound. Kennedy's head was framed by the noose of a hangman's rope, the most macabre of all the lethal weapons behind him. The whole wall was covered with trophies, as it pleased Jolly to call them, of the hundreds of investigations which Rollison had made. It was the most famous wall in London, and there were men who said that it was even more impressive than the Black Museum at Scotland Yard—for every case represented here had been handled by one man.

Rollison relaxed.

Jolly said: 'I have a little snack prepared, sir. I am sure you must be hungry,' and went out of this room to the domestic quarters, which were approached by a small passage.

'Hallo, Rolly,' Kennedy greeted, in a subdued tone. 'What happened? Are they looking for me?'

'Yes,' said Rollison, and limped again, although he was not quite sure whether Kennedy knew how freely he had moved while coming up the stairs. 'The copper you talked to was smarter than I thought.' He lowered himself into a chair, stretched out his right knee, grunted as if in pain, and went on: 'But I don't think they'll do anything more than question you. I told them everything, including the fact that you almost certainly had no time to do any harm at Park View.'

'Nice of you,' said Kennedy. He looked rather pale and drawn, and his eyes seemed huge, partly because he was tired. Rollison glanced at a small clock on the wall over the mantelpiece; it was now after one o'clock, and they had had a busy time. 'What do you advise me to do?'

'Telephone the Yard, say you understand they want to interview you, and where would it be most convenient,' said Rollison.

'Hmp,' Kennedy grunted. 'Er— Toff, I couldn't be making a mistake, could I? I couldn't be wrong in imagining that in spite of your kind words and the fact that you let me get away from Park View, you really want the police to go for me? I mean—you urged me to run away. That spotlights me. You now urge me to give myself up. That makes it easy for the police. Am I wrong, or is there some tortuous pattern in all this? Are you trying to get me in bad with the police?'

Rollison said, mildly: 'We seem to work at cross purposes all the time, don't we? The answer is—no.'

'I don't believe that you would do anything without good reason,' Kennedy said. 'First you advise me to do this, then you advise that. Where is the consistency in it?' When Rollison didn't answer, Kennedy went on sharply: 'Why don't you tell me right out that you don't trust me as far as you can see me?'

'Until we know the motive for all this, I wouldn't trust anyone,' Rollison said. 'Not even Kate Lowson.'

Kennedy flushed.

'That's a damned silly thing to say,' he said hotly. He finished a drink which

Jolly must have poured out for him, banged his glass down on the large, figured walnut desk, and said: 'All right. I'll go to the Yard and make my statement. If they hold me—I'll hate your guts.'

He stalked out.

Jolly appeared, almost as soon as the door closed—and Jolly was wearing a grey top coat, carrying his old fashioned straight-brimmed bowler hat, and a furled umbrella. Jolly, in fact, was just being Jolly. He raised his eyebrows in a formal inquiry: should he follow Dr Kennedy? Rollison nodded. Jolly went out, and Rollison hardly heard a sound as he opened and closed the door, and yet he could hear Kennedy's footsteps. Soon, he would know whether Kennedy had gone to the Yard or not. He went into the small, spotless, very modern kitchen. Coffee was bubbling in a percolator, and there were some succulent looking ham and chicken sandwiches, a small piece of a ripe-looking blue cheese, farmhouse butter, and biscuits.

'Bless you, Jolly,' he said aloud, picked up the tray, carried it into the big
143

room and told himself that he would not have to put too much weight on his knee, it was not so good as he had made Jolly believe. He put the tray on a small table, and started to sink into an easy chair, but before he had time to relax and start eating, he heard a sharp, grinding, screaming sound, as of a car brake being jammed on. Then there came a rending crash which seemed to shake the house.

CHAPTER 11

'Accident?'

Rollison was at the door of the flat while the sound of the crash still echoed, knee slightly painful but ignored. He pulled the door open and raced down the stairs, putting much of his weight on his left arm and the banisters. He heard someone calling out, but no door opened; at this hour most people indoors would be in bed. He heard no sounds from the street, and that seemed ominous. He wrenched open the street door—and caught his breath.

Flames were leaping up not far along the road, and already the whole street was touched with a lurid red glow. He felt the heat. He thought: *Oh, God, Jolly,* and ran out. He saw car headlights approaching and slowing down; they turned the fire a paler red. He saw the blazing mass of a small car halfway along the street, a few dozen yards away from the Rolls-Bentley, which did not appear to be touched. He saw no sign of Jolly or Kennedy. The flames were shooting out on either side. It was dangerous to push past, but he had to find out if Jolly were there; the moment of the crash must have coincided with the time Jolly had reached this spot. He held his breath, ducked, covered his face with his arms, and ran past the burning car, which had crashed into a lamp post. As he did so, there was a sharp crack of an explosion, and something struck the ground just in front of him. He felt a tug at his coat, but felt no pain.

He passed the danger spot—and then saw Jolly.

It was an almost ludicrous sight, especially in view of the intensity of his fears, for Jolly was standing upright, shoulders braced, umbrella hanging over his arm, and bowler hat on firmly and squarely. The red glow lit up his pale face and put a kind of malevolence in his brown eyes. Just by him, half sitting against the railings outside the house, was Kennedy; Kennedy did not seem hurt, either.

Rollison slowed down.

Doors and windows were beginning to open, and he did not want to talk to neighbours tonight. The police would be here at any minute, too. He turned his head, and looked towards the burning car, a little puzzled in spite of his enormous relief that Jolly wasn't hurt. Then he realised why Jolly was staring so fixedly.

The driver must still be inside.

* * * *

'All I can say, sir,' said Jolly, half an hour afterwards, 'is that I heard the car coming rather more quickly than I thought it should. The engine seemed to start up immediately behind me. As you have so rightly advised me, I took evasive action against the likely contingency. I also shouted to Dr Kennedy. He promptly took evasive action, too. But for that I am quite sure that one of us would have been run down. The—the alarming fact was that the car burst into

147

flames the moment it hit the lamp post. The driver could have had no chance at all.'

'I see,' said Rollison, heavily.

Kennedy was back in the big room, with another, larger drink in his hand. Jolly, at Rollison's insistence, was sitting on an upright chair—and sitting well back on it. Two policemen from the Yard were taking notes. Outside, the ambulance men and the firemen were busy, and there was a continual background of noise; metal being banged, men shouting, cars moving to and fro. But there was hardly any glow from the burned-out car, now.

'Exactly where was the car when you looked round at it?' asked one of the Yard men.

'About thirty yards along the street.'

'Did you see the driver?'

'I caught a glimpse of him, that was all.'

'What made you think that he would try to run you down?'

'I really didn't make such a statement,' denied Jolly, with great dignity. 'I simply stated that I took evasive action against the possible contingency that I would be run down. Obviously, the crash could have been accidental. The car could have been out of control.'

'No,' said Rollison, suddenly. He gave a swift, bleak smile. 'No, it wasn't out of control. A very peculiar business, indeed. Jolly, did you see the car when you first went out of the house?'

'A car was parked at the far end of the street, sir.'

'Lights on?'

'Yes, sir.'

'Engine running?'

'No, sir—at least, I didn't hear it.'

'When did you hear it?'

'Very suddenly—when I first looked round,' Jolly answered.

'Yes. That's the queer thing—it didn't have a chance to warm up, it seemed to start absolutely from scratch doing a hell of a bat,' Rollison said, and moved towards the window, and threw it open, then leaned out. Jolly and the others could just hear what he was saying. 'Did you see anyone else in the street, Jolly?'

Jolly joined him.

'I didn't quite hear you, sir.'

149

'Did you see anyone else in the street?'

'I *did* see a man some distance along.'

'Near the car?'

'Opposite it, on the other side of the street.'

'Ah,' said Rollison, and leaned further out of the window. A ring of firemen had gathered round the smouldering wreckage, and the car was little more than a heap of twisted plastic and metal. A crowd of fifty or sixty people had gathered, and was being kept at a distance by a cordon of police. At least a dozen cars were now parked further along Gresham Terrace. Rollison heard a man say clearly:

'We won't need an ambulance for *him*. An urn, more likely.'

Rollison drew further back into the room. He was looking very pale, his eyes were unusually bright, and there was a different air about him from anything Kennedy or Jolly had seen that night. Jolly, who knew his every mood, was quite sure that Rollison felt that this was a moment of great crisis.

'Anything worrying you, sir?' asked the Yard man who did most of the

150

speaking.

'Yes,' answered Rollison, promptly. 'Yes, there is indeed. I want to see if Superintendent Grice is in.'

'He isn't on *duty,* sir,' the man said.

'I'll call his home,' said Rollison, and limped to the large desk and dialled the home number of the Yard official whom he knew best, a man who was not only one of England's foremost detectives, but almost a lifelong friend of the Toff. He was aware of the puzzled expression in Kennedy's eyes. He heard the dialling tone as he squatted on a corner of the desk. It went on for what seemed a long time, and eventually a man broke it with a gruff:

'Grice here.'

'Ah, Bill,' Rollison said. 'I'm sorry to turf you out of bed, but...'

He talked for forty seconds.

Forty minutes later, tall, rangy, broad-shouldered Grice stepped into the room, a brown-clad man with brown hair going slightly grey, with a rather sallow skin which was exceptionally clear—and which was stretched very tight at the bridge of his nose, so that it was almost white. He was really too lean. There was nothing to suggest that he had just come out of bed, for he was immaculate. He had a word with the two Yard men, and sent them off obviously to their great reluctance.

'Now, Rolly, make it worth while,' Grice said. 'My wife doesn't like you very much as it is.'

'Sorry,' said Rollison bleakly. 'I never like coming between husband and wife. Bill, first things first: Mike Kennedy was on his way to the Yard to make the statement your people want from him. Let's have that established.' Kennedy nodded and murmured something. 'This car crashed into the lamp post just behind him,' Rollison went on. 'It was travelling on the far side—the wrong side—of the road. It reached fifty or sixty miles an hour in a few seconds from a standing start. Anyone at the wheel must have known that it was suicide to drive like that. But there's another thing. If a driver was suicidally inclined, if a driver did get as near Kennedy and Jolly as this car did, why did he miss? The car was apparently under control. Five yards

152

in a different direction and it would have got both men. Why didn't it? And would any driver really sit cold-bloodedly at the wheel of his car knowing that, on impact, it would blow up and burn like matchwood?'

Grice didn't answer, at first. Kennedy spoke under his breath, but no one took any notice of him. Outside, there were the raised voices and the sound of car engines, but nothing else.

Grice said at last: 'I think I see what you're driving at, Rolly.'

'That's a lot more than I do,' Kennedy burst out. 'What's all the mystery about? Why are you behaving as if this were something from another world? There was a driver. I saw him. Jolly saw him. There isn't any doubt about it. He may not have realised what was going to happen—he may even have lost control, you can't be so certain as you pretend to be. What's the mystery?'

'Mike,' Rollison said, as if casually, 'Maurice Holmes was one of the chief sales executives of Malling Motors, and as he was in the United States for two years, Malling Motors put a lot of trust in him. He came home for special consultations. We know that, although all details of the kind of consultations were missing from the papers, as far as I could judge. The point is that they were special consultations, that obviously he had information of importance—possibly of vital importance. Also, he was worried. He had something "new" to sell to the States, but we don't know for certain what it was. I think we can start guessing. A car which would drive itself—and could also be driven under remote control. I have never believed that there was a driver in that car—I believe there was a dummy. There was no smell of burning flesh at any time. If I'm right, then it was a car which could drive itself—and could be guided under remote control. If this is the hush-hush business which brought Holmes over, then it's fabulous. As for the crashed car—it might have been controlled by the man whom Jolly saw, further along the street. Whoever it was, the control was good, but not absolutely accurate. The controller made the car come to the spot where he judged you ought to be—not where you were.'

Rollison paused.

'Could be, Bill?'

'It certainly could be,' Grice agreed.

'And so you think Holmes was kidnapped because he knows all about some new kind of car?' asked Kennedy, in a low-pitched voice. 'Or do you—' he broke off. 'I know one thing, I'm right out of my depths. Mr Grice, do you really need a statement from me tonight? What with one thing and another I feel as if I could go to sleep on my feet.'

'Provided you stay here for the night, and talk to one of my men first thing in the morning, you can have your sleep,' Grice conceded.

'Thanks,' said Kennedy, gratefully; there was no doubt that he looked fit to drop. After a few perfunctory goodnights, Jolly took him along to the spare room, leaving Grice and Rollison together in the big room. Grice, nearly as tall as Rollison, was fingering the noose of the hangman's rope, rolling it between his fingers.

'Is he tired or is he scared?' Grice asked, thoughtfully.

'My question, too,' said Rollison. 'Sometimes I think he's leading me right up the garden, and at other times I think he's exactly what he makes out to be—a good doctor and a bit of an ass in everything else. My turn to know one thing, Bill.'

'What's that?'

'I'm really tired,' Rollison answered.

Grice laughed...

* * * *

The only thing Rollison waited up for was to allow Jolly to change the bandage on his knee. Already the cut had lost its anger, and he did not think that it would be much to worry about. He was asleep within five minutes of getting into bed, and slept dreamlessly, but when he woke a little before eight o'clock, his mind began to hum with all the questions which had been in it the night before. He had none of the answers yet, his subconscious had not greatly helped during the night. The problem of Mike Kennedy remained, but he set this aside as a secondary one. He knew that Grice would make sure that there was no release of the "remote control" theory, but as soon as the wreckage was cool enough, someone would discover whether there had been a driver or a robot in control; and once that reached the newspapers, it would be a week's sensation. At ten past eight Jolly came in with his tea tray, announced that Mr Kennedy was still asleep, that he, Jolly, had telephoned Miss Lowson's apartment and been told that she also was still asleep, and that Grice had telephoned at five minutes to eight.

'That's what woke me,' Rollison said. 'Give me time to drink one cup of tea, and then get him for me.'

'Very good, sir,' Jolly said.

'What's the mess like in the street?'

'Very nearly cleared away, sir.'

'Fine,' said Rollison. He drank his weak morning tea and almost as soon as he had finished the cup, heard the faint ting of the telephone bell; Jolly had a genius for perfect timing. A moment or two later, Grice was on the other end of the telephone.

'Yes, Bill?'

'Rolly, two or three things quickly,' Grice said. 'In the first place, I've made sure that the laboratory keeps everything they discover about that body quiet for the next twenty-four hours. We needn't fear any leakage of information. In the second place, I've had a word with Birdie'—Dr Willison Camper-Bird was the chief Home Office pathologist—'and after a quick check he says he doesn't think we'll find any human remains. In the third place, I've had a preliminary Fire Department report that the car was made of a new kind of plastic which is highly inflammable and of course shouldn't be used in car manufacture at all. In the fourth—'

'Let me *breathe,*' begged Rollison.

Grice laughed. 'Don't tell me you're slowing down! I've also had a talk with Meer, of the R.P. Division—you seem to have made a hit with him.'

'You watch Meer, he'll take your job one day,' warned Rollison. 'I've breathed.'

'The fourth thing is that I think that it would be better for you, not me, to go and see Malling Motors,' Grice said.

'We'll have to get round to it, but if we make too much of a song and dance it might be given the wrong emphasis— and knowing you, it's possible that you'll be able to dig out some facts which we could build on. Can you see them by ten o'clock?'

'I certainly can,' said Rollison. 'Have you identified the girl at 40, Park View yet?'

'No,' answered Grice. 'Her handbag was missing, and there was no name we could find. Neighbours don't know her. The house was supposed to be let furnished to people named Thompson.' After a pause, Grice asked: 'Do you know her?'

'Not yet,' Rollison said. 'Will you let me have a photograph?'

'Yes,' promised Grice. 'I'll send it round right away.'

CHAPTER 12

Malling Motors

At five past nine, Rollison was leaving the flat. Kennedy was awake but not yet up, and Rollison had told him where he was going. By the time he reached the street, he knew that his knee was going to be stiff, but not too painful. He wished he had asked Grice what the man with the nose pushed to one side had said, then consoled himself by thinking that if the man had talked, Grice would have told him. The police seldom refused to be co-operative, now; happy days! He was smiling to himself when he saw a Yard detective officer standing on the other side of the street. Some roadmen were trundling along with bitumen and flints, to patch up the hole which had been burned in the road, and a few men were examining the spot—probably police chemists. Rollison found that the paint at the nose and front wings of the Rolls-Bentley, now in the garage, had blistered a little in the searing heat of the fire; the marvel was that there was no more damage. He started the engine at a touch, and drove not to the Bickley Square headquarters of Malling Motors, but to Gillivry Street.

Outside stood a policeman in uniform and a little, perky man wearing a battered trilby, and sporting a suit with the shoulders too square and the waist too shapely, a pair of purple socks and a purple tie. They were talking together, but straightened up as Rollison approached, and the perky man greeted:

'Didn't think it would be long before you turned up, Mr Ar. 'Ow's tricks?'

'Nicely, thanks,' said Rollison amiably. 'How are things here?' He smiled at the constable, a youthful looking, earnest man.

'The grapevine tells me that the young lady woke up around eight thirty, and she's okay,' answered the perky man, who came from Bill Ebbutt's training establishment in the Whitechapel Road.

'The rozzers have took a statement.'

'They didn't lose much time.'

'Cor blimey, if I took as long to write me name as they do I'd go back to school,' the perky man said and grinned cheekily at the earnest policeman. 'Mr Ar, the officer and me is having a little argument. He's got the pecooliar idea that the Arsenal is a team as can play *football*. I've told him that where *football* is concerned, as apart from kick and rush and break your opponent's neck if you get arf a chance, there's only one team in it—that's Chelsea. As a fair-minded man, who do you say, Mr Ar?'

'I'm unfashionable,' Rollison declared. 'I root for Fulham.' He went into the tall house, and by the time realised that at least a dozen neighbours were staring at him from windows in the street. In the house which was well served by daylight with tall windows on each landing, doors began to open and curious people peered at him. He reached the top floor, and found two men there, one a constable, one a larger product of Ebbutt's gymnasium, sitting on hardwood chairs obviously brought out for the occasion. The constable saluted and the Cockney said:

'Watcher, Mr Ar!'

'Is Miss Lowson on her own?'

'Yes, sir.'

'Thanks,' said Rollison, and tapped on the door. A moment later, Kate answered him, hesitated for a moment obviously without recognising him, and then backed into the room. She looked rested, and she looked quite lovely; it was shocking to think that she had been within minutes of death last night. She was wearing a red housecoat, high at the neck. Some pink tulle beneath the collar high up to the chin not only hid the bruises, but had a softening effect. She hadn't made up, but had done her dark hair; any woman who could look a beauty in circumstances like these really was one.

She closed the door, and said: 'Mr Rollison, I shall never be able to tell you how grateful I am. I know that I owe you my life.'

'Yes,' said Rollison, gently. 'I think you do.' He took her hand. 'The frightening thing is that there might be other

163

attempts, Kate, and I'm here to try to find out why. Is there anything at all that you didn't tell me last night?'

He had given her every chance to dissemble, no chance to prepare for this attack. He held her hands very tightly. She felt cold. The shock of the attack still lay heavily upon her, and from the look in her eyes he judged that she was touched with the horror of the recollection. His words were calculated to do nothing but help; rather, to make that horror worse, to frighten her into telling him if there was anything else she knew.

She said very huskily: 'I've told you absolutely everything, Mr Rollison. If there was anything else, I would tell you without a moment's hesitation.' She paused for a moment, but before he could speak, she went on: 'The police say they haven't found Maurice. Have—have you?'

* * * *

Rollison told her the truth, and she said very little in response. He questioned her about Maurice Holmes's letters, and

164

tried to find out if Holmes had told her anything about the purpose of his visit to the States, or the unexpected return journey, whether he had given her any clue as to the nature of the problem. She was quite sure that he had not. The only noticeable thing in his letters, Kate now admitted, was that towards the end of the previous year, they had seemed to get shorter and perhaps to be less affectionate.

'But I couldn't really be sure of that,' she insisted. 'It was rather as if—as if the distance was making emotions fade. For a few days after I knew he was coming home I could hardly realise it. Then—well, then I read all those letters again, and began to ask myself whether he could feel just as deeply as ever, and even —even whether I did.'

'Do you?' asked Rollison.

Kate said, pressing her hand against her forehead: 'I hardly know what to feel or to think, Mr Rollison. There's been so little time. All I know is that I'm frightened in case any harm has come to him.'

'I can imagine,' Rollison said. 'It's

certain that he was alive, and probably unhurt, until late last evening.' He told her why he thought so, and watched the expression in her eyes—of relief quickly followed by anxiety. 'Kate,' he went on, 'what do you know about his uncle, Jeremiah Whittaker?'

'Not—not very much, really.'

'Did you know him?'

She said, with a rueful laugh: 'Well—yes and no. I visited the house several times before Maurice left for America, of course, and the old man seemed all right then. He made me promise to go and see him at least once a week while Maurice was away, and I did go—twice.' She forced a laugh. 'I've never met anyone quite so brazen. He simply couldn't keep his hands to himself, and he seemed to think that he had a kind of equal rights with Maurice! He was—well, a lecherous old man, I suppose, and yet it wasn't possible actually to *dislike* him. I used to telephone him occasionally, and told him this was as near as I proposed to get to him again. He thought that a huge joke. Every week, a bottle of wine arrived here with a single red rose and an invitation to go and have dinner with him!'

Rollison said musingly: 'So Uncle Jeremiah had some nice qualities and a sense of humour. Has Maurice a sense of humour?'

'Not the same kind as his uncle,' Kate answered.

'Did you know that his uncle's house had been let furnished to some people named Thompson?'

'Let *furnished?*'

'Yes.'

'Well, I'm not surprised in a way, Maurice asked me to book at the hotel instead of going straight to the house, but I assumed that was because he thought it better not to go straight to the empty house. The estate hasn't been cleared through probate for long,' Kate went on. 'The house belongs to Maurice, of course, and I would have thought he would let me know if he'd intended to let it.' She hesitated, and then added as if to convince herself: 'Of course he would.'

'Do you know anyone named Thompson?'

'Not that I remember,' Kate answered,

167

after a pause.

'Have you ever seen this girl?' inquired Rollison, and took out the photograph which had arrived just before he left his flat. He saw Kate tighten her lips as she studied it, and suspected that she knew that she was looking at the photograph of a dead woman.

'I saw her last night at the airport,' she said at last. 'That was the girl holding the dog which knocked me over.'

'Ah,' said Rollison. 'Thanks, Kate. May I use your telephone?' As she motioned towards it he went across, dialled the Yard, and asked for Grice. Kate stood looking at him, and he appeared to be taking little notice of her, but in fact he was studying her expression all the time. When Grice came on the line, Rollison said:

'The girl was with Flat Nose at the airport last night, Bill. He talked about his sister. I think you might get something out of him if you let him know what's happened. If you'd like some help—' he broke off, half smiling.

'He's due here at noon for questioning,' Grice said. 'If you're through with

168

Malling Motors by noon, why not come along?'

'What name does he give himself?'

'Bennett.'

'Hm,' said Rollison. 'Thanks, Bill.' He rang off and stood tapping the telephone with the edge of the photograph, and was not surprised when Kate Lowson asked in an uneasy voice:

'Is that girl dead?'

'Yes,' Rollison answered bluntly.

'Is it the girl who was found strangled at a house in St John's Wood last night? There was a news-cast about it on the radio soon after I woke.'

'The same girl.'

'And at Maurice's house?' Kate said, in a whisper. 'Mr Rollison, what *is* happening?'

'We're finding out just as fast as we can,' Rollison assured her. He slipped the photograph into his pocket and went on: 'Are you thinking of going out this morning?'

'I think I'd be wiser to stay in.'

'Do just that,' urged Rollison. 'Stay here until the police or I tell you that it's all right to go out. You needn't worry about anyone who calls to see you, the police and some friends of mine are on the doorstep, but—stay in,' he repeated. 'Look after yourself, Kate.'

He went towards the door, and as he did so, heard a man hurrying up the stairs, and a moment later recognised Mike Kennedy's voice as Mike spoke to the policeman on duty at the landing. Rollison glanced at Kate. Her eyes lit up as she recognised the voice, almost as much as Kennedy's lit up when he saw her.

'My, it's good to see you!' he greeted, and took both her hands. He glanced at Rollison, but from that moment on seemed almost oblivious of him. 'Well, if nothing else you owe me a good night's sleep!' he exclaimed. 'Now, tell me...'

Rollison left them.

Twenty minutes afterwards, a parking attendant at Bickley Square performed a miracle and found room for him to park the Rolls-Bentley almost outside the showrooms of Malling Motors Limited. In a doorway opposite was a man from the Yard, and another plainclothes detective was studying the several models in the big windows. The small, sleek, beautifully designed Malling Wizard, the company's most popular car, was represented in three different colours. Its larger brother, the Malling Magician, was there in two colours. In a corner was the latest Malling, the Flash. The car which had crashed and burned up in Gresham Terrace had been about the size of a 8-horse power Flash.

Rollison spent two minutes studying the cars, then went into the doorway at the side of the showrooms, to find a large entrance hall, two lifts, two attendants, and large selections of literature about Malling cars. He asked for Mr Wedlake, was taken up to the fourth floor and received by a nice-looking brunette dressed in a skin-tight dress and whose hair was brushed smoothly back from her forehead.

'Have you an appointment, sir?' She gave him a professional smile which could not hide her interest.

'Not yet,' Rollison said. 'Tell him that I've come to see him about Maurice Holmes, will you?'

'Mr *Holmes!*' the girl exclaimed, and

was shaken out of that slick professional aplomb. 'Do you know where he is? He was due to see Mr Wedlake last evening, but didn't arrive. It's extremely important that he should attend a conference which is being held in Watford this afternoon. *Do* you know where he is?'

'Do you know where Mr Wedlake is?' asked Rollison mildly, and handed her his card. On one side there was the simple announcement of his name and address, but on the other was a skilfully drawn design—of a top hat set at a jaunty angle, a monocle, a cigarette burning from a holder, and a bow tie; in fact it was a drawing of a man without a face. The girl glanced down, saw it, and exclaimed:

'So there *is* something wrong!' She leaned forward, pressed a button on a telephone, and a moment later said: 'Mr Wedlake, the Toff is here to see—' she broke off, as if in confusion, and corrected herself quickly: 'I mean, the Honourable Richard *Rollison* has called to see you, and he has some news of Mr Holmes.' There was a moment's pause, and then she said: 'Yes, sir, right away.'

She put down the receiver, stood up, and said: 'Will you come this way?'

CHAPTER 13

Wedlake

It was a long, narrow, panelled office. The carpet was a wine red colour, and Rollison's feet seemed to sink into it. On each panel was a painting of a girl getting out of one of the Malling cars; the artwork was beautifully executed, and the faces and the pictures had almost household familiarity. These were the original drawings of the illustrations for Malling advertisements. Long windows on one side of the room did not let in enough daylight, and concealed-lighting shone on the high ceiling. At the far end of this office was a large desk, fairly close to the wall.

Behind the desk sat Mr James Wedlake, the sales director of Malling Motors.

Wedlake stood up as Rollison entered.

He was a burly red-faced, powerful-looking man, and his face had at one time been as familiar as those on the walls, for he had been a racing driver of remarkable success and colourful reputation. The years and probably much whisky had taken their toll, but there was something reckless about him, something aggressive in the way he stood up, said, 'All right, Chloe,' then rounded his desk and came forward with a big hand outstretched. 'Mr Rollison—I don't know whether to say I'm glad to meet you, or that I wish you to hell out of here!'

His hand could have crushed Rollison's, had Rollison been unwary. As it was, he gripped very tightly, and then let go.

'We ought to find out pretty quickly,' Rollison said, mildly.

'Do you know where Holmes is?'

'I only know that he's disappeared.'

'Any mystery about it? I mean, anything that would normally bring you into it as a private eye?'

'Yes.'

'Now I know I wish you were to hell

out of here,' declared Wedlake, and grinned; he had rather big, yellowish teeth. 'No offence meant, but you do trail trouble around, don't you?'

'Yes.'

'What—' Wedlake began, and then flung a hand towards a deep easy chair, and went on: 'Sit down, and tell me all about it. Mind if we have a tape recorder on? I'm going to have to report to the board this afternoon. I don't know what we've done to deserve a bloody turn-up like this, but—' He was moving about all the time, and suddenly pressed a switch; immediately there was a slight humming sound. 'The microphone's concealed,' he explained, and promptly pressed a button on the telephone, snatched up the receiver, and barked: 'Coffee, Chloe, quick.' he rang off, and sat against the side of the desk. 'I suppose we ought to start where you come in.'

'Or we ought to start with where you do,' countered Rollison. 'Why was Holmes brought back in a hurry?'

'For normal business consultations, that's all. He's been away two years, and that's long enough. We've got our main annual sales conference next week, and we've got to have an up-to-the-minute report on the American sales position before—'

He broke off, astonished, for Rollison, having sat down, eased himself to his feet, and picked up his hat and stick. He beamed at Wedlake, and had the satisfaction of rendering the sales director completely speechless.

'Good morning,' he said, politely. 'I don't know whether it's been nice knowing you or not.'

Wedlake exploded: 'Where the hell do you think you're going?'

'Home.'

'Are you mad?'

'Oh, no, not mad. Just not sufficiently gullible.'

'What are you driving at?'

'Holmes seems to be in some kind of trouble, Malling Motors seems to be in some kind of trouble, one or two people on the wings have been caught up in that trouble, but we won't get anywhere if the Malling Motors policy is one of the big lie,' explained Rollison precisely.

'Are you calling me—' Wedlake

seemed unable to get the words "a liar" out.

Rollison was halfway to the door.

'Nothing personal about it,' he declared, 'but I know and you know that Holmes was summoned because of some kind of emergency reason. Something's up. I'm far too busy to be pushed around, so—'

He was near the door, but before he could touch the handle it opened, and the sleek girl appeared, carrying a silver tray with coffee and biscuits; she looked startled at the sight of him so close to the door, more startled when she looked over his shoulder towards her employer.

'Put that down and shut that door,' Wedlake ordered. 'Rollison, let's stop fencing. You're quite right.'

'Ah,' said Rollison. 'Thanks.' He moved back to his chair, still limping more than necessary, put his hat and stick back, and saw how astounded the girl was. Wedlake was beginning to grin, and it gave him a ferocious appearance; the bark of a laugh which followed as the door closed was in keeping with such ferocity.

'Beginning to believe what they say about you,' he declared. 'All right, we'll play it your way. If I can't answer your questions because of policy reasons, I'll say so. Anything I tell you will be the blunt truth. Holmes was sent for for emergency consultations.'

'Why?'

'Complications with American distribution of a new and secret Malling model.'

'What complications?'

'That's a policy question which I can't answer.'

'Let's see if I can,' said Rollison, musing, and Wedlake stopped in the act of pouring out coffee, and looked round sharply. Rollison stretched out his legs, and went on, musingly: 'Holmes was in the States to work on the distribution of a new Malling model, probably to be called the Guided Missile. He had a very specialised and important job to do and certain parts of it were under conditions of absolute secrecy. I imagine that he supervised the distribution for the standard Malling models, the Wizard, the Magician, and the Flash, but his real job was with the secret model. Recently, he—or you—have had reason to believe that the secret is out. You were relying on hitting the American market for six with it, provided you had absolute secrecy. Now you're not so sure you can get it. I suspect that you believe the leakage could have sprung from Holmes, hence the summons. No sugar, thanks.'

Wedlake hadn't yet poured out the coffee, but stood there, neck twisted round, utter incredulity on his big features and in his rather close-set eyes. He moistened his lips, was about to speak, checked himself, poured out coffee, and brought a cup across to Rollison and handed it to him. His big right hand was a little unsteady, as if he were suffering from a kind of shock.

'Thanks,' said Rollison, politely.

Wedlake gulped. 'How did you find out all that?'

'Guesswork and some luck.'

'I don't believe it.' Wedlake gulped again. 'You must have access to confidential files, you—' He broke off. 'You've got this from Holmes!'

'I've never met Holmes.'

'Then it's utterly impossible, unless you've had access to secret correspondence.'

'I haven't had access,' said Rollison softly. 'Holmes was spirited away from the airport last night as if by one of your Wizards. He hasn't been traced. His brief-case was found, with some correspondence and some documents in it, but I saw nothing that looked confidential. If there was anything, it was taken out.'

'Good heavens!'

'And we don't know where it is or who took it,' said Rollison.

'It's unbelievable,' Wedlake muttered, and gave a passable impression of a caged animal as he began to walk up and down the room, one bunched fist smacking into his open palm. 'He was due at my house last night, at half past eight. When he hadn't arrived by ten o'clock, and—' he broke off, and stood squarely in front of Rollison, demanding roughly: 'How do you know these things?'

Rollison said: 'He was met at the airport by Kate Lowson, his fiancée, but she was prevented from seeing him. I was asked to try to find him on her behalf. One thing followed another. She was attacked, and nearly killed. A man named Bennett was arrested and charged with attempted murder. A girl who might be Bennett's sister was found strangled. A dog was killed.' Rollison brought all of this out smoothly, and then slid the photograph of the dead girl out of his pocket. 'Do you know her?' he inquired.

Wedlake stared for a long time, before he answered.

He said: 'Yes, I know her—and I know her brother.' He closed his eyes, as if the realisation was painful, and then swung away from Rollison and leaned against the desk again. 'Bennett used to work for us. He started by driving cars to and from the works to our distributors, and became one of our key salesmen. We had to dismiss him, two years ago. We—' he straightened up again. 'Do you say his sister was *murdered?*'

'If that is his sister?'

'This Bennett the police arrested,' said Wedlake, gruffly. 'Is he a man of medium height, dark-haired, nose broken and flattened?'

'Yes.'

'That's the man, so that's his sister,' Wedlake said, and his voice became hoarse. 'Did they have anything to do with Holmes's disappearance?'

'Yes.'

'I knew it,' Wedlake said, and suddenly crashed his fist on the big desk. 'I knew that man was utterly unreliable! We brought out some modifications in our Magician two years ago. The modifications appeared on two other manufacturers' models almost at the same time. I was sure there was a leakage of information, and it was thought that this was from the technical staff, but I never trusted Bennett. He was one of the few salesmen who knew what was coming along, and he always seemed to have more money than he should have had. Lots of people liked him, though. Attempted murder, and—' Wedlake seemed to boggle at the next words.

'Was he fond of his sister?' inquired Rollison.

'I would say so, yes. He was a pretty gay spark, never settled down, had a different girl-friend whenever he could use the 'fluence. In fact I used to see him at expensive restaurants and nightclubs, that's what first made me suspicious. We introduced another modification, and laid a trap for him—he fell right into it. He was selling out to a small firm of engineers who passed off the modifications to the other manufacturers as their own. Bennett went out on his crooked neck.'

'So he would hate your guts,' murmured Rollison.

'He might well do,' agreed Wedlake. 'He might—' the big man broke off, and went on in a voice which was almost choking. 'Yes, he was the type who would do anything to get even. He still has friends in the offices, too, he's got a clever tongue.'

'Could he have known that Holmes was coming home?' Rollison asked.

'Oh, he'd prise that out of someone at the office,' Wedlake answered.

'Then probably Bennett fixed Holmes's disappearance—unless Holmes knew he ought to be wary of him.'

'Holmes would know Bennett had left the company but wouldn't be likely to know the whole circumstances,' said Wedlake, heavily. 'No reason why Holmes shouldn't go off with him, if Bennett was at the airport. And Holmes had most of the details of the new Rocket—' he broke off, and a faint shadow of a grin appeared at his full lips. 'You got the name wrong, we're calling the new model Rocket, not Missile. We—but how did you know we had this new model with that *kind* of name? Supposing you tell us that, Rollison. No one outside the very small number of development engineers have had anything to do with it. The development men are absolutely trustworthy. No model has yet appeared outside the factory—it hasn't been given an open road test yet.'

'There was one in London, last night,' Rollison objected.

'Oh, no, there wasn't,' denied Wedlake. 'It's physically impossible. There are only a dozen models, all of them in our Watford factory. Just what are you trying to do, Rollison? Are you trying to tell me that you know everything about the Rocket, and want paying to keep quiet?'

CHAPTER 14

Rocket

Rollison put down his coffee cup, leaned his head on one side, and answered Wedlake mildly:

'No. I'm not going to break your neck for that silly talk either. How difficult would it be to manufacture a Rocket?'

'Without our technical knowledge, practically impossible on an economic basis. It's a question of mass production, of course. That's how we're planning to launch it.' Wedlake rubbed his red neck vigorously. 'You know so much about it that I suppose there isn't any point in keeping anything back. We planned to put ten thousand on the market almost overnight. We've special storage facilities, huge warehouses all over the country and the United States. Holmes has been arranging for assembly in

Canada, as a matter of fact. The car looks like an ordinary 10-horse power model, and there are skilfully spread rumours about a new one on the way. The special control equipment can be fitted in afterwards—in fact that's been our biggest headache, making a model which could be adapted, as it were. The car can be operated by remote control, for getting it out of garages, parking and awkward spots, but its chief quality is that it's almost accident proof. It is operated by rays which enable it to take evasive action, so that collisions are very rare. It's the answer to car damage, road accidents, the lot, and once it's in mass production it will sweep the market. The Malling Evasion System will be needed for every other make of car, too. We've done a magnificent job, Rollison. Until this trouble arose in the States, we were practically set to go. I don't mind telling you that it's worth a fortune for Malling Motors, and will give a hell of a lift to the nation's export trade. If the idea is stolen, it can be disastrous. Why, we've pent half a million pounds in research!'

'Wedlake,' Rollison began, and then

described exactly what had happened in Gresham Terrace the previous night. He saw the other's face pale beneath the criss-cross of purple veins, and could tell that Wedlake was deeply worried. He began to walk about the office again, as Rollison went on: 'The police know about it, and before long the fact that there wasn't a driver will be in the newspapers. There are two ways of dealing with that—pretending that a driver was seen to leap out before the crash, or letting the newspapers get the remote control story. Once it leaked out, it would make the evasion system seem pretty weak, wouldn't it? This car *did* crash.'

'That would be ruinous!' Wedlake exclaimed.

'You'll have to convince the police of that before they keep it from the Press,' said Rollison drily.

'We can convince the police all right,' said Wedlake. '*You're* our problem—you and the people who have kidnapped Holmes. *Kidnapped Holmes,*' he repeated, as if that were the only way to make himself believe that it had really happened. 'When we tell the Ministry of Supply how this could affect the export drive, they'll fix things with the Home Office quickly enough. As it won't stop the police from doing their job, there can't be any objection.' He seemed to be talking himself into that belief, and added abruptly: 'Don't you agree?'

'You're probably right,' conceded Rollison. 'Could a Rocket be home-made, so to speak?'

'Do-It-Yourself stuff?' growled Wedlake. 'Given the components, yes, I suppose so. This thing was made of stuff which burned like celluloid, so that's probably what it was made of, and it could be made to crash, you know. Easy to make by hand, like any racing car. An old chassis would do, and almost any old engine, all that's needed is a complete set of the control equipment and the know-how to use it. Any good electronics man would be able to set it up one he had a model to work from. Rollison, that's a line to follow up! You want a good electronics man, a garage where there's a lot of experimental work on cars, usually that's a garage owned by someone

interested in motor racing—no one
thinks twice about an unusual car or
equipment at those places. We know
Bennett's been associated with this, and
he was a racing driver at one time. Had a
crash and got out. He never did have any
guts.' Wedlake seemed prepared to
believe that anyone with less physical
courage than he had was a coward. 'Can
you get moving on that? I don't mind
telling you it's worth practically anything
—anything—to make sure that we find
out who is behind this leakage, and stop
it from doing injury to the company.
You can name your own fee.'

'Very tempting,' Rollison said, 'but
I'm in this for Kate Lowson.'

'Oh, Holmes's girl,' Wedlake said,
scornfully. 'Makes hats, doesn't she.
What do you think you'll get by way of
payment from her? A couple of Paris
models?' He gave his aggressive grin
again. 'I've that board meeting this afternoon. I'm quite sure that the board
would agree with me—you can name
your own fee. Why not say ten thousand
pounds,' suggested Wedlake. 'That's
enough even for the Toff, isn't it?'

'If we start talking terms I'll put you in touch with my man Jolly,' Rollison said, mildly. 'Just at the moment, I'm concerned with the Rocket. Can I see one in action?'

'Why should you?'

'Call it part of my fee.'

'It will take an hour to drive to Watford, and—'

'I can spare the time,' Rollison said, 'provided I can make a telephone call first.' He stood up, and limped towards the desk as Wedlake said: 'Help yourself.' Rollison lifted the receiver and a girl answered him almost at once; Wedlake made sure of very quick service. 'Whitehall 1212,' he said, 'and ask for Superintendent Grice, please.' He held on, while Wedlake stared, standing there with his great shoulders hunched and his fists clenched. 'Hallo, Bill,' said Rollison. 'How would you like to postpone talking to Bennett, and come up to Watford for an hour?...Yes, right away...Yes, some facts, and we could talk as we go...I want you to meet Mr Wedlake, anyhow. Anything new in?...Pity.' He rang off, and smiled amiably into Wedlake's startled face. 'Just to make it nice and official,' he said. 'Shall we go in your car or mine?'

* * * *

It was a little after twelve-thirty when Rollison and Grice drove into the miniature racing circuit at the Malling Plant. This was a part of a few thousand acres of rough land, criss-crossed with narrow, paved roads; the testing circuit where everything could be done with absolute privacy. In one section there were dozens of parked cars, and Wedlake drove towards these. Two other men were waiting there, a small, grey-haired, grey-moustached man introduced as Colonel Bilston, and a youngish, sharp-featured man, Mr Carmichael; both were members of the Malling Motors board.

'Everything has been laid on,' Colonel Bilston said, after they had greeted one another. 'No doubt Mr Wedlake has already filled you in with the details of the purpose of this new type of motor car, gentlemen.' He spoke rather like a man addressing a public meeting, shoulders squared, hands clasped in front of him. 'It is of course the greatest advance in motoring ever known. At last we have an automobile which can be controlled, as a guided missile can be controlled, from any given point—by a passenger who might be called a driver, or by any person standing within fairly easy range. The value of the car cannot be over-estimated. It takes evasive action when at a certain proximity to metal, thus greatly minimising the risk of collision. It has a crab-wise wheel movement which makes parking a pleasure instead of a nightmare. The Rocket can park in a smaller space than any other car. It is extremely manoeuvrable. The system of electronics built into it is such that on the open road it can be used without a driver, for it needs only to be set on the right road and will adjust its own direction. However, a demonstration will be much more convincing than any amount of talk. Would you care to climb on to this observation platform, gentlemen?'

He stood aside. The wooden steps leading to a nearby platform, a kind of watch tower, were very strong. Rollison and Grice went ahead. Wedlake followed, Colonel Bilston came ahead of Mr Carmichael. When they were standing on the platform, Colonel Bilston said:

'Do you see the small pale green car, by the right of those tree stumps, gentlemen?'

'Yes,' answered Rollison, and tried to sound unconcerned.

'You see, there is no driver,' Bilston pointed out. 'Here is the control mechanism—quite small, you see. It can be built into the car itself, or it can be used from any convenient place. The range of control is limited so far—no more extensive than about a radius of a hundred yards—but that is all that is needed in present conditions. The car—but perhaps you should have been allowed to examine it before we start it in operation!'

'We'll examine it afterwards,' Grice said, and glanced at Rollison as if to say: 'Do you believe any of this?'

'Very well,' said Bilston, and picked up a small egg-shaped object, rather like an electric switch. Rollison saw him squeeze it. On the instant, there was a roar of sound—the kind of roar Jolly must have heard the previous night. The car shot forward from a standing start at unbelievable speed, and stopped almost as abruptly. Then the colonel put it through a series of gyrations which had to be seen to be believed. The car weaved in and out of other cars which were stationary on the road. It turned circles. It made U-turns. It stopped opposite spaces which seemed too small for it to go, and crept, sideways, into the parking position. Finally, the colonel sent it on to a small circuit, and let it go all out. The harsh noise faded, the engine was almost silent, and Rollison judged that the car travelled at sixty miles an hour without changing its path at all. Then he saw that part of the circuit was like a huge turntable, and stationary cars on it began to move. The test car appeared to be hurtling straight at one, swerved, swerved again in front of another, swung round to avoid a third.

Throughout all this, Grice was staring round-eyed and with parted lips, and Rollison's eyes began to glisten. He knew that the directors of Malling Motors were watching them both, and saw that the colonel's hand went slack as the little green car came back to the spot from where it had started.

No one spoke, until Grice said:

'If you can put that on the market in any quantity, it will be a world-beater.'

'*Now* you understand our deep concern,' Colonel Bilston said, with gloomy satisfaction. 'We have financial interests supporting us to an unlimited amount of money. At one time we considered floating a new company and inviting public subscription on the strength of our very considerable reputation, but we came to the conclusion that a few private investors were, in fact, more likely to be what we required.' Once he was started, the colonel seemed unable to stop talking, and words spilled out from him. 'Had we invited public subscriptions it would have been difficult to explain exactly why we required so much capital, whereas with private investors fewer explanations were necessary. We gave them demonstrations, and let them into one of the main secrets, a treatment of steel and aluminium which repels all metals at a certain proximity. After all, Mr Rollison, would *you* hesitate to invest in such a project as this?'

'If I were a rich man, no,' Rollison said.

'You are rich in friends and rich in acquaintances, reputation, and influence,' said the Colonel. 'However, that is beside the point. I was about to add—'

'Who are your big financial supporters in this?' inquired Rollison, thoughtfully.

'That is a confidential matter, of course, and I do not see how it affects the issue in the slightest degree,' said Bilston. 'If you, superintendent, were able to say that you needed the names of those individuals and corporations who are investing in this remarkable development I would divulge them after an opportunity for full consultation with my colleagues, but for the time being I hope you will agree that it is superfluous.'

Grice nodded.

'Thank you. The vital thing, of course, is to find out who has been able to get access to the prototype, and to create the model which, it appears, was used last night. Holmes was coming back because he told us that two or three American interests—one of them a financial supporter of our project—have reason to believe that there has been a leakage of the information, and it is *possible* that at least one American car manufacturer will soon be able to compete. Holmes was to give us full details. That is why it is absolutely essential for us to find him, and talk to him.'

'How much information could he give away if he were under pressure?' demanded Grice.

'A very great deal,' the colonel answered. 'In fact Maurice Holmes has become a key man in our activities. We have depended absolutely on his loyalty. We cannot, obviously we cannot, be so assured of his physical courage. A man under threat of pain or death might easily divulge information which he would otherwise treat as confidential—as, in fact, a sacred trust. Mr Rollison—superintendent,' went on Colonel Bilston with great earnestness, 'I have no hesitation in saying that upon your finding Maurice

Holmes depend many matters of supreme importance.'

He paused, raised a hand, and began to count with his right forefinger thrust outwards towards Grice.

'*First,* to ourselves, as individuals. All of us have sunk our personal fortunes in the Rocket.

'*Second,* to our shareholders, who are many, and among them are comparatively humble people whose interest from our shares is a major source of income.

'*Three*, to our employees, many many thousands of them, who enjoy conditions of work and privileges second to none in the motor industry—in fact, in industry of any kind.

'*Four,* to our country, because of the almost incalculable value of the export sales which would undoubtedly follow upon the launching of this revolutionary motor car.

'*Five,* to the cause of humanity, because so many road accidents would be avoided.'

Bilston paused again, and then turned to face Grice, glancing at Rollison as he did so, before going on:

'Find Maurice Holmes for us, gentle-men. So very much depends upon it.'

CHAPTER 15

Bennett

It was a little after three thirty when Rollison and Grice turned into the gateway of Scotland Yard, driven by a chauffeur in a Rolls-Royce with a glass partition which had enabled them to talk without being overheard. They had said very little on the return journey, after Wedlake, Bilston, Carmichael, and two other directors who had arrived for the afternoon conference had given them an excellent lunch in the directors' restaurant at the works. One after the other, the directors had urged the vital importance of finding Holmes, and between each plea, Colonel Bilston had made some earnest comment.

The car pulled up at the front of the steps and the two sergeants in the hall saluted as Grice and Rollison walked up.

Still silently, Grice led the way to his office, on the third floor. It overlooked the embankment, where the green of the trees was restful and beautiful in the afternoon sun, which bathed the Thames in diamonds. Traffic was humming past, and now and again there was the reminiscent sound of a noisy engine. Grice lifted a telephone, and said:

'Is Bennett still across at Cannon Row?...Right. Have him brought across to me in twenty minutes.' He put down the receiver, smiled a little wryly at Rollison, and said: 'I seem to be able to hear Bilston talking all the time.'

'The never ceasing record-player,' Rollison murmured. 'I should hate to sit on a board meeting with him. It would always go on for hours too long. Bill—'

'Yes?'

'I think I would like to find out the names of the men who are putting their money into the Rocket.'

'Might be wise,' agreed Grice, and rubbed the shiny bridge of his nose. 'If one of them has large interests in another car-manufacturer, it might pay him to sell Malling's out. Is that what you think?'

'It's obviously possible,' answered Rollison, 'and I'd like to know anything that Bilston and the others would like to keep to themselves, anyhow.' Grice nodded, and after a pause Rollison went on: 'I can still hear that car engine starting up—from zero to fifty miles an hour like—'

'A Rocket,' Grice finished for him, drily.

Rollison chuckled. 'You're getting too quick for me, it's becoming quite a police habit. Bill, if Bennett will talk, we might be well on the way with this job. He's obviously a tough customer, and he's an old hand at racketeering. The odds are that he won't make any statement to you, even if you do shock him into realising that his sister was murdered.'

'Whereas, you think, he might be persuaded to talk to you,' said Grice, and spread his hand. 'Rolly, I don't disagree, but there isn't a thing I can do. There have been times in the past when I've wanted to crack your skull because you whisked someone away and talked to him when you should have handed him over to us, but the years taught me that

you could often get information that w~
couldn't. But the day hasn't dawned
when I can turn a man over to you for
questioning.'

'You—ah—you could be called out of
the office as soon as he's brought in,'
Rollison observed, straight-faced. 'If I
happened to be on my own for five
minutes with him, it might work
miracles.'

'He would know that as you were here,
we were working together.'

'That's quite likely,' agreed Rollison,
and put his right leg up on a chair, as if it
were causing him pain. 'Bill, would five
minutes really do any harm? I mean,
supposing the Assistant Commissioner
did know what you'd done, would he
complain all that much?'

'I wish I knew what you've got up your
sleeve,' Grice said. 'Have you been
thinking this out on the journey? I've
never known you quiet for so long.'

'I was suffering from a surfeit of
Bilston's gaff,' said Rollison. 'Five
minutes, Bill.'

'Do you seriously think you can make
him talk?'

'Yes.'

'Will you pass on everything he tells you?'

'Yes.'

'Before you leave here, I mean, not after you've been able to act on what you learn.'

'Yes.'

Grice laughed.

'I've never known you a bare-faced liar,' he conceded. 'I'll see what I can do. Keep quite for five minutes, will you, I ought to look through these reports.' He pushed cigarettes across the desk, and Rollison took one and lit it, and then stood up and looked out of the window at the sunlit London scene. It was quite beautiful, with the diamond-studded river reflecting the sky, and some craft on it moving very slowly and gracefully, Westminster Bridge with several scarlet buses on it, and the great block of the London County Hall across the river. Further along was the square shape of the Festival Hall, and the sweeping arches of Waterloo Bridge. He studied all these in turn, but was not thinking about them; they acted as a kind of stimulant to his thoughts, and he had never thought more quickly than he did now.

Grice said: 'Right, Rolly, thanks.'

Rollison turned to face him. 'Anything new?'

'Nothing at all. Nothing was found at the addresses you got. The name of the girl was discovered just after we left London—it's June. Apparently she and her brother lived at 40, Park View. We haven't yet found out where they lived before going in there. There is one thing: before the estate was settled the solicitors in charge gave permission to Holmes to let off the house, furnished to some people named Thompson. The rent, fifteen guineas a week, was a useful contribution towards the general expenses of clearing up the estate. That's reasonable enough.'

'Was it reasonable that Holmes should do it without letting his fiancée know?'

'I don't see why not,' Grice argued. 'There are plenty of men who keep all their business affairs from their wives. I wish—' he broke off, when his telephone bell rang, lifted it, announced himself, said: 'Right,' and put down the receiver at once. 'Here's Bennett,' he announced. 'Do something for me, Rolly. Don't say anything for the first five minutes.' He lifted the telephone again, and then said: 'In ten minutes time, give me a single ring on this telephone will you? There was an echo-like sound of the operator saying: 'Yes, sir,' followed instantly by a sharp tap at the door.

Rollison was standing behind the door, in a position where he could see but not be seen immediately. Grice was standing behind his desk.

'Come in,' he called, and the door opened and Bennett appeared.

Rollison saw the way his dark eyes glittered, saw the set of his full lips. The flattened nose spoiled his looks and, with his jaw thrust forward and his teeth obviously clenched, gave him a savage look. He was of average build, and just now he moved very slowly and deliberately. He turned his head, as soon as he had seen Grice.

He saw Rollison.

Rollison didn't speak.

Grice said: 'All right, sergeant, leave

him and stay just outside the door.' He waited until the man went out, leaving Bennett framed against the door. Whatever else was true, this man's spirit hadn't been crushed. Rollison moved to a chair, and sat down with his foot up on a window ledge. Grice motioned to a chair in front of the desk. 'Sit down, Bennett.'

Bennett neither moved nor spoke.

'Please yourself,' Grice said, 'but you won't help anyone by behaving like a surly fool. And you won't help yourself by refusing to talk. Your associates haven't shown you or your sister any consideration. It's time you realised that if you're going to get a square deal it will be from us, and not from the people you work with.'

Bennett didn't speak.

Grice said, evenly: 'What are the Thompsons now, and who are they?'

It was like talking to a blank wall.

'Bennett,' Grice said, with the patience of long experience, 'we don't mind whether we take two hours, two days, two weeks or two months to break you down. You'll break. You've attempted

208

to murder a woman, and that will see you in prison for a large slice of your life, unless you can prove that you had extreme provocation, then it could be a short period. Or,' he added, almost casually, 'if you can prove that you were under any kind of pressure or coercion.'

Bennett stood, stiff as a sentry outside Buckingham Palace; he did not seem to move even an eyelid.

Grice glanced at Rollison.

'He's been like this ever since we brought him in, Mr Rollison.'

'Struck dumb,' murmured Rollison. 'It was a pity I didn't have ten minutes with him alone. That's the trouble with the law, it's so gentle.' He paused, and added: 'The murdering so-and-so.' He paused again, and Grice was looking at him; now Bennett shifted his gaze a little so that he could see Rollison, although he tried to pretend that he was looking straight ahead. 'To do a thing like that,' Rollison went on softly. 'It was one of the most vicious things I've ever come across. It must have hurt like—'

He stopped.

Bennett was gritting his teeth.

Grice said: 'Agonising.'

'And the dog first,' Rollison said. 'That would have been bad enough. It looked as if it had been in convulsions. God! If I had the killers here—'

Bennett turned round to face him, eyes glittering and lips parted, and for a moment it looked as if he were going to speak. But he did not, and with a great effort of will, he made himself stare past Rollison and out of the window. There was utter silence for several seconds before the telephone bell jarred out. Grice was playing this game extremely well; no one could have been more co-operative. He let the bell go on ringing, and that made Bennett turn his head, as if the noise were getting on his nerves, and making them raw. The bell went on and on. Bennett drew a deep breath, and shouted:

'Why the hell don't you stop that noise?'

Grice stared at him, and then very slowly stretched out his right hand, lifted the receiver and, still looking at the prisoner, put the instrument to his ear.

'Grice speaking.'

There was a pause.

'Yes, sir,' he said, and there was a slight inflection in his voice; there seemed no doubt that he was speaking to a senior officer. 'Yes, right away. Er—I needn't be long, need I?' There was another pause. 'Thank you, sir.' He put the telephone down, and stood up, slowly, with Bennett still glaring at him. 'I've got to nip along to see the A.C.,' he announced. 'I won't be more than five minutes. The sergeant will be outside the door if you want anything, Mr Rollison.' He went out, rather slowly, and Rollison could well believe that he was hesitant because of what he was doing, not just because he wanted to increase the pressure on Bennett. If anything went wrong, and Bennett escaped or even made an attempt to escape, Grice would be blamed for allowing the prisoner to stay there without a police guard.

The door closed on Grice.

Rollison turned and looked at Bennett, then slowly stood up. He took out cigarettes, and held his gold case open in his hand, but he did not go nearer the prisoner or proffer the case. He took his time about speaking, and he felt sure that the self-imposed silence was now almost more than Bennett could bear.

He asked, softly: 'Can you remember what it was like to feel Kate Lowson's neck beneath your fingers, Bennett?'

Bennett moistened his lips.

'Do you remember how she struggled and how she heaved?' asked Rollison. 'Do you remember what it was like when she seemed to stop breathing, and when it looked as if you'd killed her?'

Bennett was gritting his teeth and clenching his fists.

'Because you ought to remember,' Rollison said. 'That was what happened to your sister. Only no one saved her.'

Bennett actually backed a pace, raising his hands in front of him, as if to fend off some physical thing. Rollison stood absolutely still, with the case open in his hand, his face set with unusual gravity. He heard the other man's harsh breathing, and felt sure that he would soon begin to talk.

'Exactly what happened?' Rollison went on. 'She must have—'

'You bloody liar!' Bennett screeched

at him, and leapt at him bodily, teeth showing as his lips turned back, lean, lithe body coming like a catapult.

CHAPTER 16

Talk

Rollison had judged the moment when the other man would spring, and he did not need to move. He slid the case into his pocket and shot his right fist into Bennett's stomach. As the man gasped and lurched forward, head lowered, he clipped him sharply beneath the chin, then rammed his fists to the man's heart —all blows which would hurt, but none likely to put him out. Bennett tried to cover up, but could not, and he banged against the wall. Rollison struck him twice again, sharp hurtful blows to the stomach; then he backed away.

'The truth is the truth. They killed June like that,' he said harshly.

Bennett was gasping for breath.

'Exactly as you tried to kill Kate Lowson,' Rollison went on. 'Like some proof?'

He moved to Grice's desk, and picked up some of the photographs, selected one which had been taken of Bennett's sister simply for the pathological department's use. He turned it round and handed it to Bennett, whose gaze dropped. Sweat was standing out in little globules on his forehead, and on his clean shaven upper lip.

'No!' he gasped.

'Ugly way to die, isn't it?' said Rollison, icily.

'God, they wouldn't—'

'They did. They poisoned the dog, presumably because the dog would have tried to save her. Then they strangled her. How much do they deserve your loyalty?'

'It—it must have been someone else.'

'Stop fooling yourself,' Rollison said. He did not glance towards the door but heard footsteps in the passage, and was afraid that Grice was coming back. He wanted a few more minutes alone with this man; the sight of Grice might yet stiffen his resolve. 'Are you in this to ruin Mallings?' he demanded.

'Ye—yes,' Bennett muttered. 'Partly.'

'What made it worth trying to kill any-one?'

Bennett didn't answer.

'Listen, Bennett,' Rollison said reasoningly, and he held out the cigarettes, 'what you've got to understand is that you're utterly friendless. 'You're probably penniless, too—don't you realise that?'

'I—I suppose so.'

'No matter how much you hate the Malling people, they aren't worth hanging for,' Rollison said. 'Why did they drive you to attack Kate Lowson? Who is this Thompson?'

Then Bennett answered in a way which made Rollison believe he was telling the truth—and was perhaps the biggest single disappointment Rollison had known for a long time.

'I simply don't know,' Bennett muttered. 'It's just a name he calls himself. I don't—' he closed his eyes, and for a moment it looked as if he would faint. Rollison took a brandy flask out of his hip pocket, unscrewed the cap, and handed it to Bennett, who took a drink eagerly, and was gasping when he

216

lowered the flask. 'It's the truth,' he muttered. 'I don't know who Thompson is. I do know that it isn't his real name. His Christian name may be, though—Lancelot.'

'Can you describe him?' asked Rollison.

'Yes,' Bennett answered, 'but—but it won't be much good. He always wore a beard, and—well, I always thought it was false. He kept a scarf on, and—well, he never seemed real, if you know what I mean.'

Rollison thought: It's getting almost like a music hall sketch. But there was nothing remotely comic about the expression in Bennett's eyes. The man gave the impression that he was only now beginning to absorb the shock of the news of his sister's death. He brushed a hand across his forehead, and went on:

'He did it so that we shouldn't recognise him. He—he was a man of middle age, I'd recognise his figure and his walk, but his face—' he broke off, and stepped towards Rollison: 'Rollison, you're not lying to me?'

'I'm not lying,' Rollison said, quietly.

217

'I wish I were. Who else was in this with you?'

'He had—he had two other men with him,' Bennett answered. 'They lived at Park View, too, a man named Bell and another named Carby.' He shivered. 'Oh, God, it's hard to believe that—' he broke off again. For a moment it looked as if he were going to break down and cry, but he fought against that, and when he went on his voice was stronger: 'I'll tell you everything I can, Rollison. I'll help in every way I can.'

That was when the handle of the door turned, and Grice came in briskly; obviously he had been standing outside the door. He nodded to Bennett and Rollison, and made no comment when Bennett dropped into the chair which he had refused before.

'Bennett's going to give us all the help he can,' Rollison said. 'No need for a shorthand writer yet, is there?'

'No,' Grice conceded.

'Bennett, let's get one or two things clear,' said Rollison. 'What was your sister's part in this?'

Bennett closed his eyes as he answered:

'That's the worst part about it. She knew who Thompson was. She worked with him before I did. He was supposed to be—to be in love with her. I never liked him. I never liked—'

He had not liked many people for a long time, Rollison decided, watching the man; Bennett had lived with a chip on his shoulder for months, perhaps years. Grice was sitting back and watching, not taking notes. Neither of them prompted the man, who took another sip of the brandy, then a cigarette which Grice pushed across the desk.

'It really began because I hated Wedlake's guts, and everyone at Malling Motors,' he said. 'I was accused of selling out some manufacturing secrets. It was a cold-blooded lie. I gave Malling Motors everything I could, I was absolutely loyal to them—and they kicked me out at a moment's notice, with a month's salary.'

'Do you know who did give those secrets away?'

'No, I couldn't even guess, unless it was that swine Wedlake himself,' Bennett answered. 'I wouldn't trust him as far as

I could see him, but—well, what use was there in accusing a director? I don't mind telling you that I could have cut Wedlake's throat. I think if I'd seen him the week or so after he'd slung me out, I would have done him an injury. The hell of it was, I was in debt even when I was at Mallings. I daresay I'd been a fool to overspend, I was getting a fair salary—but not as good as you might think. Mallings are the meanest so-and-so's in the business. They say that they have to screw everyone else down in order to offer the public the cheapest possible product, but the truth is they're bloody mean and bloody-minded.'

Rollison nodded: Grice was looking almost smugly satisfied.

'Well, I had nearly five hundred poundsworth of debts, and was really in trouble. My—my sister knew about it, too. She fiddled about a bit at secretarial work and made enough to cover her own expenses, but I couldn't get any money from her. Then Thompson offered me this job.'

'Did she work for Thompson at the time?'

'Yes. She'd been a kind of part time secretary to him, and suddenly he wanted to expand.'

'What kind of work did he do?'

'He called himself a general agent, dealing mostly with export of machine parts and cars, mostly to the tropics,' Bennett answered. 'I never did know much about the job. I do know that I did a bit of driving for him, delivering some cars to the ports—and afterwards I discovered that the cars were stolen. He told me that provided I did whatever he wanted I needn't worry, but that if I kicked over the traces, he'd report it to the police.'

Rollison murmured: 'The old blackmail story, Bill.'

Grice nodded.

'Old or not, it had me in a devil of a fix,' muttered Bennett. 'He'd paid me good money, and—well, what's the use of lying about it?—I knew that I was getting more than the job was worth, and realised there must be something fishy about it. I just didn't want to believe it, until it was too late. The worst of it was, he seemed to have got June on the same kind of racket—she was selling stolen furs and jewellery.'

Neither of the others spoke.

'I was in it so deep that I began to see it as normal,' went on Bennett. 'It didn't seem to me that I was doing anyone any serious harm—mostly the insurance companies were suffering. Then Thompson gave me a chance to work against Malling Motors, and I wanted to do that more than anything I've ever wanted to do in my life. I hated the sight and sound of them. If I saw a Malling car going along the street I wanted to spit on it. You may think I'm unhinged,' he went on, bitterly, 'but the injustice of it rankled all the time—it was like a canker.'

'I can imagine,' Rollison said.

'It was only last week that Thompson told me that there was a chance of getting my own back on Malling Motors. He'd been told that Holmes was coming back from America to report, and said that he wanted to talk to Holmes about certain aspects of the American market.' Bennett closed his eyes again and pressed his hands against his forehead and it seemed a long time before he went on: 'Thompson told me that he'd just given June her job, then offered me mine, and got his hold over me because he wanted someone who knew Mallings inside out. He said that if he could find out the secret of the new Malling model he could probably make a hundred thousand pounds by selling it to other manufacturers, and that would cost Mallings plenty. I fell for it hook, line, and sinker. It was exactly what I'd longed to do. We laid on the job of getting Holmes away from the airport. It was a bit tricky, because we realised that Miss Lowson would almost certainly be at the airport, and there was a risk that someone from the company would be, too. June and I went along, with Tig.'

'Tig?' asked Grice.

'Our dog,' Bennett explained, huskily. 'We've had him for over five years. He was an R.A.F. dog, and I knew a chap who arranged to put them out to grass, so to speak. June was always a bit nervous on her own at night, and so we got Tig. God! To think that she—'

Again, it looked as if Bennett would

223

break down, and again he overcame the emotion, and went on:

'We laid it on carefully. When we knew that no one from Mallings was going to the airport—Thompson got hold of that—it seemed easy. We had intended to prevent Miss Lowson from getting to the airport, there—there was to be an accident, she—she would have been badly hurt. But at the last minute our plan went wrong. Another car baulked—baulked ours, so we had to make emergency plans. They worked perfectly. Holmes knew that I'd left the company but didn't know why, you see. While Miss Lowson was unconscious, I told Holmes that she had been delayed through illness, and that I'd been asked to take him to see her. He came like a lamb. I took him to Park View, and he hardly put up a fight, he was so shaken.'

'What did Thompson want from him?'

'A lot of documents about the new Malling project, and all the information he could give,' Bennett answered. 'I wasn't at any of the sessions. I was never anything more than a kind of ball-boy.

These other men were with Holmes, and I believe they gave him a pretty rough time. Then—well, then Thompson told me that I'd got to kill Miss Lowson.'

'Why?'

'Look,' Bennett said, desperately, 'I can't tell you what I don't know, and I don't *know* why. Can't you understand the situation? Thompson had me where he wanted me. He didn't explain or argue, he just told me what to do. He wasn't difficult provided I ·did it—I'd learned that a long time before. He said that it was vital to his plans and our future to kill her and make sure she couldn't identify me; she had to be killed, and that I had the job to do.'

Grice leaned back in his chair.

'And you agreed—just like that?' he asked, incredulously.

Bennett eased his collar, pushed his chair back, and then suddenly stood up. The way he began to pace the room reminded Rollison of Wedlake in that long, narrow office not very far from here.

'I know what you're thinking, and God knows I can understand it, but the truth is, I was desperate. I knew I was a criminal—don't you understand that? I'd become a habitual criminal, too. If the truth of all the things I'd done came out, I knew I'd probably spend the best years of my life in prison. I might even spend more. I was terrified of the very idea. The thought of it could drive me into a panic—it always could. From the first time that Thompson threatened to tell the police what I'd been doing, I felt it. It—it was like a phobia. I would do anything, anything at all, to save myself from going to jail. I used to hate myself for being such a gutless fool, *but I couldn't help it*. And—and then I realise what it was,' he added, hoarsely. 'I realised that Thompson and my sister between them had broken my spirit. It was like a drug. I—I could no more refuse to do what Thompson told me than I could refuse to eat or drink. And I—I told myself that if I didn't do it, someone else would. I couldn't save the woman. There was Thompson's other man, the one who was sent with me— named Carby. We were to do it together. Carby came with me, to keep watch. I knew that if I didn't kill Miss Lowson, he would come up, and—God, I've told you, haven't I? I hadn't the guts not to. I hated myself for what I was going to do, and yet I knew that I couldn't avoid doing it. When I look back now, it's like remembering a nightmare, and yet I would have killed her. I'm not pretending that I wouldn't, I would have killed her.'

He broke off, sweating freely. Grice moved his chair back, and Rollison shifted his position so that Bennett could get up and move towards the window. It seemed a long time before anyone spoke again, and then it was Rollison who asked, quietly:

'Bennett, do you know what they propose to do with Maurice Holmes?'

'As soon as they've got all the information they want from him, they'll kill him,' Bennett answered.

CHAPTER 17

Cause for Alarm

Bennett seemed to be absolutely sure of himself, and neither Rollison nor Grice spoke for several seconds. Bennett stopped pacing the room, stretched out towards the cigarettes on the desk, but hesitated as he asked: 'May I?'

'Help yourself,' Grice said, and as the man lit his cigarette, he went on:

'Are you quite sure of this?'

'Thompson made that clear all along,' Bennett answered. His eyes held a desperate look, and he drew in the smoke as if his life depended on it. 'It's no use going half measures. I knew that murder was intended. I'd drilled myself into agreeing, and—' he gulped. 'There was another reason why I didn't find it so hard as I should. I hated Holmes as much as I did Wedlake.'

'Why?'

'Holmes got this American job, which I wanted. I'd practically been promised it, two years ago, and then Holmes got it over my head.'

'Do you know why?'

'When I was fired, Wedlake told me that I'd lost the American job because I was suspected even then of selling Malling's out—but it wasn't true. Someone may have made the board think I was, but if they'd really given me a chance to defend myself, if they'd told me when they first began to suspect, I could have proved that I wasn't working against them.'

So the chip had been on his shoulder for about two years, Rollison realised, and was partly due to Holmes getting this plum of a job.

'Did Thompson say he meant to have Holmes killed?' asked Grice.

'For the same reason that he said Kate Lowson had to be. Holmes knew me, and if he gave me away to the police I might be able to give a lead to Thompson. I'm as sure as I can be that Thompson killed June because he wanted to make sure that no one could give him away. He knew I don't know for certain who he is.'

'Have you any idea?' asked Grice.

'No, I haven't the faintest. But Thompson knew June had, although she would never tell me. He'd always warned her that we would run into real trouble if she did, and—well, since she'd known Thompson, June wasn't the easiest person in the world to handle. She changed absolutely. All she seemed to care about was money and expensive clothes. I suppose the truth is that each of us had all it takes to be a criminal even before we realised it. Thompson must have known that.' Bennett's eyes were burning, as if he had an almost unbearable headache. 'If I had the faintest idea who this Thompson really is, I'd tell you.'

'What general description can you give us?' asked Grice.

'He's my kind of build, about my height, too,' Bennett answered. 'I should say I'm slightly taller. He's an older man, too, I should say—probably in the middle-forties. He's got a small scar in the back of his neck, just behind the left ear, about an inch long, as if he'd had a nasty jagged tear there at some time. He's dark-haired, and the beard was obviously a false one—he never made any attempt to hide that fact.'

'And can't you give us any indication where to find him?' asked Grice.

'Absolutely none at all.'

'What about these men, Carby and Bell?'

'You saw Carby,' Bennett said to Rollison. 'Bell is a taller, thinner man, in the early forties I'd say. They're both pretty tough, although they're not up Thompson's street in any way. They're non-commissioned types, and Thompson's what we usually call a gentleman.' There was bitterness in that sneer. 'God, my head feels as if it's going to burst! Can I have a couple of aspirins or something?'

'I'll lay some on,' Grice promised, and pressed a bell. 'A bit later, I'll get you to dictate this statement and then sign it, Bennett.'

'Oh, I won't close up again,' Bennett assured him. 'I thought my only hope was to say nothing at all. I knew if I once started to talk it would all come out. Er—I suppose I ought to say thanks to you both for treating me like a human being.'

'Forget it,' Grice said.

When Bennett had been taken out, and the sergeant with him briefed, Grice walked to the window and looked out for several seconds, one hand deep in his trousers pocket, the other resting lightly on the window ledge. When he turned round, he was smiling faintly, although there was a shadow of anxiety in his eyes.

'That's how far fear will drive some men,' he said. 'I ought to hate the sight of him, but instead I almost felt sorry for him.'

'I shouldn't waste your pity,' Rollison said, heavily. 'But I know what you mean.'

'You worked that trick all right, anyway,' Grice went on. 'Now we've got to judge where it takes us.'

'Not near enough to Thompson or Holmes,' Rollison said gloomily.

'No. I've a feeling that Bennett's right, too—that Holmes will be murdered when he's told Thompson all he knows. We haven't a clue to Thompson's identity, either.'

'Distant clues, surely,' said Rollison, more thoughtfully. 'Holmes knows him. Find Holmes, and—' he broke off. 'All right, all right. There's another man on Thompson's list if we can believe the signs.'

'Dr Kennedy?'

'Yes. It isn't reasonable to believe that last night's attack was on Jolly. Jolly couldn't have known anything,' Rollison said. 'Kennedy seems to be in danger from Thompson, whatever the reason. Bennett might be right when he says that Thompson ordered him to kill Kate Lowson because she could recognise him again, but there could have been some additional reason which Thompson didn't speak of.'

'Just what is on your mind?' demanded Grice.

Rollison said, softly: 'I think we ought to take it for granted that Kennedy, Kate Lowson, and Holmes are all in danger, and that there might be more attacks on Kennedy and Kate. If there are, it will be because each of them can help us to find Thompson. Right?'

'You could be.'

'Thanks,' said Rollison, but obviously his mind was racing. 'I asked Ebbutt's chaps to keep an eye on Kennedy, and I warned Kate not to leave her flat until we've given her the all clear. I think I'll go and see her again, now. She might know more than she realised, and it's even possible that she knows more than she wants to tell us.'

'Don't dream up too many suspects,' Grice advised. 'I wish—'

He broke off when the telephone bell rang, and swung towards the desk. He plucked up the telephone, announced himself, and then his manner brightened and he picked up a pencil and bent down to make notes. 'Good—yes, I'm ready, Mr Wedlake.'

Rollison tried to catch what Wedlake said, but although his voice came clearly into the room the words were not easy to hear. Grice wrote swiftly, and Rollison watched over his shoulder. He was making a list.

Arthur B. Morhead
Simon Assen
Sir Mortimer Bailey

He finished writing, Wedlake's voice boomed distantly, and then Grice said:

'No, we haven't anything else yet, the moment we have we'll tell you. Thank you again, goodbye.' He rang off and straightened up, and there was a gleam in his eye as he looked at Rollison.

'You can guess what they are, can't you?' he said.

'The three financiers who've backed the Malling Rocket.'

'That's right,' said Grice. 'The only three, too—I gather they've put up half a million pounds each. Rolly, I can get all the detailed information necessary, but why don't you go to see each of these fellows?'

'I will,' promised Rollison. 'Before the night's out, too, if I get half a chance. Check that they're in England—'

'They are. Wedlake tells me that they're having a joint meeting with the board tomorrow afternoon. They had to be kept advised of developments.'

235

'Ah,' said Rollison, and stood absolutely still for a moment. He did not realise that while Grice was eyeing him he was also reflecting that the years touched Rollison very lightly; there was something about Rollison's face and manner which gave him a distinction even greater than when he had set out on his legendary, almost unbelievable career. And Rollison had no idea that in that moment, too, Grice was reflecting ruefully that there was no man he liked better than Rollison, and probably no man at the Yard who had as keen a mind. He knew Rollison better than anyone else did, except of course Jolly. He was quite sure that ideas were flashing through Rollison's mind which would probably be scoffed at by the average Yard man, but might hold the vital clue to the mystery of the Malling Rocket.

Rollison relaxed.

'Solved it?' Grice asked, mildly.

Rollison looked startled. 'Er? Oh, no!' He grinned. 'As I told Meer, I leave that kind of thing to policemen. I have just had a hunch.'

'I thought so.'

'Holmes may know this Thompson. Kate Lowson probably knows him. He operated from old Jeremiah Whittaker's house. Was that by chance? Could Thompson be associated with the Holmes and Whittaker families? Was there any other heir to part of the old man's estate?'

'There was a cousin—sorry, a nephew —of the old man's who got five hundred pounds and a dozen bottles of port,' Grice answered. 'He hasn't been traced, as far as I know—I talked to the solicitors handling the estate only this morning about him. He was last heard of in South Africa, I gather he was a bit of a roamer. You might have something; it's worth checking, anyhow. What are you planning to do next?'

'Go and see Kate Lowson,' Rollison answered.

'You don't seriously think that she's in danger now, do you?' asked Grice. 'I'm much more worried about Holmes. I'll put out a general call for Carby and Bell, and see what descriptions I can get from Bennett. How well did you see the man Carby?'

'Fairly well. Forty-ish, heavily-built, powerful, nasty,' Rollison recited. 'I shouldn't be too sure that we needn't worry much about Kate.'

'If you think it's necessary, we'll double the guard,' Grice said.

'Might be wise, especially by night,' Rollison agreed, and smiled suddenly and expansively. 'Thanks, Bill. One day I'll have to join the C.I.D. or you'll have to resign and come into partnership with Jolly and me.'

Twenty minutes later he turned into Gillivry Street, and almost at once he saw another, different prize-fighter from Ebbutt's Gymnasium, and another, different policeman from the one who had been on duty that morning. These two were not on arguing terms. This policeman was a younger man who had an aloof manner, and Ebbutt's man, a well known cruiser weight with forty-odd victories to his credit, simply winked.

On the landing were two more men.

'Everything all right?' asked Rollison.

'Nothing to report, sir,' said the policeman. 'Dr Kennedy came in about twenty minutes ago, otherwise there have been no visitors.'

'That's good,' said Rollison, and tapped at the knocker.

There was no immediate answer.

He did not feel any sense of alarm, and in fact felt that there were indications that Grice was more right than he about danger to Kate Lowson. The fact that she could have identified Bennett might have been a sufficient motive for murder, after all.

He pressed the bell, and heard it ring inside the flat.

There was still no response.

For the first time, he began to feel a little uneasy. Then he told himself that Kennedy and the girl might possibly have been caught at an awkward moment. Had Holmes been in here, though, not Kennedy, that would have been easier to believe. He frowned. The policeman stepped towards him, put a large forefinger on the bell push, and kept it there. Ebbutt's man, named Smith, joined them at the door. The ringing sound came clearly, but there was no answer.

'But Dr Kennedy went *in*,' the

policeman said, as if bewildered.

'Did you recognise him?'

'Oh, yes, sir, and the lady called him by his name,' the policeman reported, and turned to Ebbutt's man. 'No one's come out, have they?'

'Not while I've been here,' the boxer answered promptly, and he began to look alarmed. 'There can't be nothing wrong in there, can there?'

Rollison said: 'The quicker we get inside the better. Constable, this is where you turn a blind eye.' He took his knife out of his pocket, opened it to the pick-lock blade, and slid the pick-lock into the keyhole. He twisted for a few seconds, and then heard the lock click back. He thrust the door—but it did not open.

'It's bolted,' the boxer breathed. 'They've locked themselves in.'

CHAPTER 18

Forced Entry

The policeman sounded badly scared as he said: 'Why *should* they?' The boxer looked alarmed, as if he felt that he was somehow to blame for what had happened. Rollison drew back from the door, and said in a tense voice:

'The bigger of you two had better help me to break that door down. Smithy, will you hurry down to the chaps outside, and have the back of the house checked —there was someone watching from there, wasn't there?'

'Yes, indeed there was,' the policeman said.

'Look slippy, Smithy.'

'Oke.' The boxer ran as the policeman drew back from the door, turned his massive shoulder towards it, and said: 'Let me see what I can do, sir, no need

241

for you to strain yourself.' He went close to the door, took the handle, and thudded his fifteen stone against it; the door quivered, obviously fastened only at the top bolt. He drew back and tried again, a remarkable demonstration of controlled strength. There was a rending sound, and the door sagged. 'Once more,' the policeman said, and this time drew further back and launched himself at the door bodily. It crashed open, and he staggered inside. Rollison was on his heels, feeling a sense of alarm which drove every other thought away.

What would they find?

The large room was empty. The great north window, half in the wall and half in the ceiling showed up everything clearly. It was tidier than Rollison had seen it that morning. The bedroom door was ajar, and he pushed past the constable, but there was no one in the room, the bed was made, everything was spick and span. The constable was striding towards the doors on the far side of the room, and Rollison caught his breath, for he smelt one thing quite clearly.

Gas.

The policeman said: 'Don't strike a match.' He held his breath, and tried the handle of the door; it was locked, but made of matchboard, and he had only to throw his great strength against it once, and it crashed in.

Gas billowed gently out at them, and the policeman began to cough. Rollison saw a kettle, burned out; gas was hissing beneath it. The constable was bent almost double with coughing. Holding his breath, Rollison pushed past him. Kate Lowson was sitting on a small chair in front of the open gas stove, and Kennedy leaning against the wall, supported partly by the gas stove and partly by a dresser. Neither of them moved. Rollison bent forward, gripped Kate by the arms, and dragged her out of the room. The policeman had recovered enough to go in for Kennedy. Cool air was coming in, and Rollison carried the girl halfway into the big room, and then turned her over on her stomach on the couch; artificial respiration might be the only way to save her. The policeman came out with Kennedy over his shoulder, and the man was still coughing. There were footsteps up the stairs. Rollison raised the girl's eyelids, saw that the pupils were pin-points, realised she had had morphia, and then began to apply artificial respiration, while another policeman and Ebbutt's man came in.

The policeman turned off the gas, then strode to the telephone.

* * * *

Half an hour afterwards, both Kennedy and the girl had been taken away in an ambulance, with a non-committal doctor in attendance. Grice hadn't yet arrived, but there was a detective sergeant from the local Division, who had said very little so far. Policemen watching from the back had been questioned, but none of them had seen anyone enter the flat by a window, and everything pointed to one thing; that Kennedy and the girl had tried to kill themselves, first by drugs, then by gas.

There was another possibility: that Kennedy had drugged the girl, and she had not known what was going to happen.

His head swimmy from breathing in too much gas, Rollison did not argue with the Chelsea inspector and the police surgeon, who put this down at once as murder and suicide, or a suicide pact. Had it been Holmes, such a pact was conceivable, but unless Kennedy and the girl had known each other much more than anyone had suspected, it did not make sense.

Had they met for the first time at the airport?

Kennedy's eagerness to help, the fact that he had come to solicit aid from him, Rollison, all suggested that he had been extremely anxious for Kate Lowson. Would a man be so concerned about a casual acquaintance, even if she had a face and a figure that were quite out of the ordinary? Had he, Rollison, allowed himself to be fooled? Even if he had, even if these two are old acquaintances, what had caused this new crisis? *Had* it been a suicide pact—was there any possible reason for one?

Suicide pacts implied a state of acute depression and of mental unbalance. Rollison remembered how terrified Kate had been the previous night, and how the fear of death had affected her. Would anyone so frightened of death one day, welcome it the next?

Rollison ruled out a suicide pact.

So, the logical answer was that Kennedy had first drugged Kate into unconsciousness, put her on that chair, stood leaning against the wall watching her, with the gas streaming out of the boiling ring.

Did that make sense?

'No,' said Rollison abruptly, and saw the Chelsea inspector glance at him. The man was nearing his retirement and had a rather weary and almost doleful expression. Rollison said:

'How could anyone get in, apart from the door?'

'Talking to yourself, that's the first sign of insanity,' the Chelsea man said, almost with satisfaction. 'That window's in full sight of the garden at the back where our chaps were watching. No one came in, Mr Rollison. It's no use beating your head against a brick wall.'

'No,' agreed Rollison, politely. 'How about the roof?'

'Well, there *is* a little loft, just large enough for the water tanks,' the other man informed him, 'but you mark my words, Mr Rollison, it wasn't used for this. It couldn't have been.'

'It's worth checking,' Rollison said.

* * * *

'The truth is that you don't want to believe that Kennedy was responsible, so you won't face up to the evidence,' Grice declared, when he had talked to Rollison and the Chelsea man, and after a preliminary inspection of the loft hatch.

'That's right,' Rollison admitted.

'It isn't like you not to face facts.'

'No,' agreed Rollison, firmly. 'But I like to be sure of them before calling them facts. Mind if we check with the hospital again for the latest report?'

'There won't be any news yet,' Grice said, but he went to the telephone, dialled the Yard, and instructed them to check with the West London Hospital where the two victims of the gassing had been taken. When he rang off, Rollison was standing in the kitchen door and looking at the gas stove; then suddenly he spun round, eyes glistening, and rushed across to the bedroom. He seemed to have recovered completely from the damage to his knee. He thrust open the door, went down on his knees, and pushed up the bedspread where it fell to the floor.

Grice was just behind him.

'Rolly—'

'Bill,' called Rollison, in a muffled voice, 'come and have a look at this.' He edged himself out a little and Grice frowning, joined him on the floor; they stretched out on their stomachs, to the obvious annoyance of the Chelsea inspector. 'See,' said Rollison, and it was not often that he showed so much excitement. 'The film of dust under there has been disturbed a lot. There are some scratches on the varnished boards, obviously recently made, probably made today. Look over by the wall—the paint-work has new scratches, too. Get your chaps to go through this room thoroughly, Bill. They'll find that someone was under here and had to find a way in other than the street.'

Grice said thinly: 'No, damn it—'

'It would be possible. Whoever it was could have crept out by night. Remember that Kate Lowson was sleeping under a drug.'

'I've got to admit that it could conceivably have happened,' said the Chelsea inspector, reluctantly. 'Whether it did is a different matter. Shall I bring our chaps round to search the room, or will you send for men from the Yard, superintendent?'

'Your chaps, please,' Grice said crisply, and as the Chelsea man turned round to the telephone, it rang. Rollison watched him lift the receiver, and studied his face; he sensed that whatever else, the news wasn't bad.

'That's good,' the Chelsea man said. 'No change, then.' He put down the receiver, and in his slow way, went on: 'That was the hospital. There's no change in their condition, but they're hopeful that neither of them will die. They took morphine all right.'

'So we've got a chance of hearing what they say,' Rollison remarked, and pressed his hand against his forehead.

'Bill, talking of facing facts—it's a fact that the only people whom we know and who might be able to help—apart from Bennett—are Kennedy, Kate Lowson, the unknown Thompson and his men, Carby and Bell. Plus, of course, the Malling Motors people. Wedlake might know more about the campaign against them.'

'I suppose so,' conceded Grice.

'And here's a determined effort to make sure that Kennedy and the girl can't talk,' went on Rollison. 'If the man was hiding here before Bennett made his attack, it means that he intended to make absolutely sure about the girl. And he was here to finish off Kennedy, too.'

'If Kennedy came into this affair for the first time last night, then anyone waiting here to kill Miss Lowson couldn't have known about him,' Grice argued. 'You can't have it all your own way.'

'Good point,' Rollison agreed, and the familiar glint was in his eyes. 'Amazing how I hate the obvious today, isn't it?' He put his head on one side. 'It's also amazing that all this schemozzle went on today as well as last night, but no one in the flat below seemed to have been disturbed. I wonder if we could check that flat, Bill?'

'We can try,' Grice said. 'But there's a little thing you've forgotten. Whoever came in here—if anyone did—had to get out. You're not suggesting that anyone could have got out after you found the couple unconscious in the kitchen, are you?'

'If the man only had to go to the flat below, it could have happened,' Rollison said, and now stared down at the floor of the bedroom. 'Bill,' he went on, 'why don't you forget all about the flat below until I've tried to find out if anyone's there?'

Grice hesitated and then said:

'All right, Rolly. I've let you stick your neck out so far, a little more won't make much difference.'

Rollison went into the kitchen, collected the pepper pot, slipped it into his pocket, and left the flat, going quietly down the stairs. He could hear men talking down in the hall, and could imagine the way Ebbutt's men and the police were arguing that it was impossible for anyone to have got into the premises without their knowing; and so it was. Rollison reached the front door of the flat below, which was immediately beneath Kate's. The door looked exactly the same, too. He pressed a bell which was fastened to the middle of the door, and the ringing sounded very loud; there was a battery set on the other side of the door. There was no response; he had not really expected any. He wished that he had thought of this at a time when he could have come here without the awareness that the police were on the alert, but the police could not get a search warrant for this flat without much stronger grounds.

He rang again, and there was no reply.

He wished that he could call the policeman who had broken down the door of the upstairs flat. As it was, Grice would find it impossible to pretend not to notice if he started hammering on the door, or trying to break it down. He took out his pick-lock, and began to use it cautiously. All the locks on these flats were an old mortice type which could be picked with a skeleton key, but weren't really easy. This one seemed more difficult than that upstairs.

Rollison was very conscious of the fact that he hadn't much time.

He heard the lock click back.

He pushed gently, glancing upwards as he did so, afraid that the bolts would be shot; but the door yielded. It made little sound. He pushed it wider, and daylight came from the window which seemed to be in exactly the same place as the window upstairs. He heard nothing else. He pushed the door wide enough to step through, dropped his right hand to his pocket, and went inside.

The room was furnished with old-fashioned, Victorian furniture. It had a dilapidated look about it, too—an unlived in look. He closed the door without fastening it. The layout appeared to be exactly the same as Kate's flat, with the kitchen on the left, the bathroom beyond it, the narrow bedroom on the right.

He stepped towards this, and as he did so, he heard a movement behind the closed door of the bedroom.

CHAPTER 19

Man to Man

Rollison stepped swiftly alongside the bedroom door, close to the wall. There was another sound, and no doubt at all that someone was moving. He thought that the movements were furtive, but could not be sure. He pressed close against the wall, and the sounds seemed to be much louder. A floorboard creaked. He watched the handle of the door, and after what seemed a long time, it began to turn. It moved so slowly that there was no doubt at all of the furtiveness of whoever was there, but that did not necessarily mean that the person had no right here. It might be a man or a woman, scared by sounds in the flat; any householder would have reason to be scared.

The door opened wider.

Rollison could not see into the room. He had to wait for the door to open still more. He believed that someone was actually standing in the doorway and looking towards him; there was no way of being sure that he could not be seen. He remembered the gun which the man he had first attacked had held. One shot, well aimed, could be deadly. He held his breath as the door creaked as it opened wider. Would anyone, frightened, behave quite like this?

Then he saw the muzzle of a gun, and he was in no doubt. He flung the pot, the pepper billowed out when it struck the door; a gasp was followed by a choking kind of cry. Rollison moved, on the instant. He kicked the door wider open, saw a man reeling back, the gun waving in his hand. How right he had been! Then he saw the man trying desperately to recover his balance, and trying to point the gun at him.

The man fired.

Rollison flung himself downwards, knew that the bullet could only have missed him by inches, and clutched the man's legs with his outstretched hands.

The man crashed. He heard a shout from upstairs, and a moment later footsteps thudded on the stairs. He grappled with the man, struggling to grip his right hand, knowing that the gun hadn't dropped. He felt the cold steel. He knew that if the man could twist his hand and squeeze the trigger again, it would be fatal. He had to make him drop that gun. He clutched the sinewy wrist and tried to twist it—but the man's strength was nearly as great as his. He felt the other try to bring up a knee and drive it into his stomach, wriggled to one side, and caught the blow on the thigh. Then two men rushed in, and from that moment there was no need for alarm.

* * * *

When he looked down at the captive, a few minutes later, Rolly recognised the man whom he had attacked downstairs, whom Kennedy had left unconscious, and whom Bennett had called Carby.

* * * *

'I know,' said Grice, 'you were able to do what we couldn't. No one's going to charge you with breaking and entering. If you keep this pace up, you'll be stretched out on a morgue slab before we have a chance to charge you with anything. Are you all right?'

'The after effects of good honest fright, Bill, that's all. The bullet was a lot closer than I like.'

'It was a lot closer than I like, too,' Grice said, grimly. 'Well, let's see what we can find. I've a nasty feeling that we're going to find that you were right again,' he went on, smothering a grin. 'I shall still call it guesswork.'

'I don't care what you call it,' Rollison rejoined. 'I've just been realising how lucky I was that the men who came here last night didn't leave the guard inside the doorway. If they had—' He broke off. 'Well, it happened. Shall we try the kitchen first?'

'Why?'

'Because the kitchen floor was covered with linoleum, which is easier to push up than boards with a bedstead on it,' Rollison said.

They went into the kitchen of the downstairs flat, and needed only a glance to see exactly what had happened. There was a large hole, chipped out of the plaster of the ceiling, and showing the joists and boards beyond. Grice pulled up a kitchen chair, stood on it, and pushed against the boards; they went up easily. Light shone down from Kate Lowson's kitchen. It was a comparatively simple matter for anyone to climb up and down here.

'Not much doubt what happened,' commented Grice. 'They used the kitchen to get in and out when they couldn't use the front door, but we moved a table in the kitchen so that it wasn't possible last night. Carby had to find somewhere to hide. He hid under Miss Lowson's bed, and got out and downstairs when she was asleep.

'We can't give the men in the big room full marks, but the man only had a few feet to cover without being seen, it could be done all right.' Grice paused before going on: 'He had a telephone down here, and could be in constant touch with Thompson, and be briefed about Kennedy. The acutal method by which he drugged them doesn't matter for the moment; but it wouldn't have been difficult for him to have slipped a pill into some milk, made sure they would drop off to sleep, and then turned on the gas. That way it would stop us looking for the murderer—a suicide pact would seem the obvious answer. It was practicable all right, Rolly.'

'Yes,' Rollison said. 'And it means that they want both Kennedy and Kate dead. So, what or whom do Kennedy or Kate know?'

'Thompson,' suggested Grice.

'Could be,' agreed Rollison, and looked across at Carby, who was standing between two men, handcuffed to one of them. He had refused to say a word. 'You couldn't stretch another half inch and let me have a session with Carby, could you?' he said wistfully.

'I wish I could,' said Grice with feeling.

It was obvious that Carby simply would not talk, and as obvious that it would not be possible to find any pressure that would break him down, as

Bennett had been broken. He was a much tougher type.

When he had been sent to the Yard, Rollison was taken to Gresham Terrace by a police car. As he stepped out of the car he saw a movement at the window of his flat, and had no doubt that it was Jolly. He let himself in, and went slowly upstairs. The shock of finding the two people gassed and the swift struggle with Carby had taken a lot out of him. He hoped that no one was upstairs with Jolly, and that he could take a little time to ease the pressure, and to let thoughts drift through his mind rather than force himself to think in emergency.

The door was opening as he reached the landing, and Jolly stood there. Last time, Kennedy had been waiting inside. This time—

'Don't say we've company,' Rollison said, hopefully.

'No, not at the moment, sir,' said Jolly, 'but Mr Wedlake is calling at half past eight. I told him you would not be back until then,' Jolly added, 'although he was most insistent. I understand from one of Mr Ebbutt's men that you had been—ah—very busy, and I took the liberty of making sure that you had a little respite.'

'Bless your heart,' Rollison said, and yawned. 'Respite is badly needed, yes. First, a whisky and soda.' He stepped into the room with the trophy wall—and there was a whisky and soda already poured out by the side of his favourite chair. He began to smile. 'Then a bath,' he went on, and picked up the glass.

'The water is running, sir,' Jolly said.

'Yes, it would be. Did I ever tell you that I don't know what I would do without you?'

'I think we can agree that that is mutual, sir,' said Jolly, and a smile lurked in his eyes. 'And I thought that a mixed grill would be better for dinner tonight, as I wasn't sure what time you would be home.'

'A cheese soufflé to follow, perhaps?'

'That is already being prepared, sir.'

'Yes,' said Rollison, very slowly, 'I certainly don't know what I would do without you. You are going to be bored, too. You are going to listen to me talking. You are going to help me probe the mystery. Because there must be a CLUE! Jolly. Somewhere in the depths of the problem—' he sipped his drink, rolled the whisky round his tongue, and went on: 'Somewhere in the depths, I say, this CLUE lurks. It is something so obvious that we've all missed it, something we almost certainly know about but which has a deeper significance than we realise. Am I dithering?'

'I suspect that you have had a very trying day, sir. If I may venture to advise you, it would be wiser to finish your drink, have your bath, and try to forget what is worrying you. Perhaps a little music would help. Then after dinner, I will be at your service.'

'In other words, will I let you get on with your job,' Rollison said, and smiled. 'Yes. A little more whisky in this, and some gentle music. Gentle, soothing, music, perhaps. What would you recommend?'

'For this mood, sir, perhaps Grieg.'

'Grieg it shall be,' agreed Rollison.

It was a little under an hour before he had finished the cheese soufflé, was out of the little curtained-off dining alcove, and sipping a liqueur. He wore a dressing-gown on which the Cross of Lorraine was worked in white silk upon a dark blue silk background, he looked sleek and yet lethargic, and proposed to change just before Wedlake was due. He began to talk, using Jolly as a sounding board, going over everything that had happened in the past twenty-four hours; it was difficult to believe that so short a time had passed since Kennedy had come to see him.

At last, he finished.

'And what do you make of it, Jolly?' he inquired mildly, noting that it was nearly a quarter past eight. He was warm, cosy, and comfortable, and the thought of dressing did not attract him; Wedlake could be received in a dressing-gown. He drew at a cigarette, and studied Jolly, who at his command was sitting back in a small armchair.

'I think you are right in one way, sir,' Jolly said. 'The key mystery is, why should Kennedy be attacked? For that matter, why is it so important that Miss Lowson should be? Bennett's explanation, that she could have betrayed him and his sister no longer holds water—the attack on her at her flat makes it clear that she still appears to constitute a threat to the unidentified Thompson. As does Kennedy. I—er—have been doing a little quiet research in Dr Kennedy's recent movements, in his family and social circle.'

'Ah,' said Rollison. 'Is he the villain?'

'I have questioned fifteen people who know him well, at the airport and elsewhere, and it appears that he had no romantic attachments,' announced Jolly, precisely. 'As far as it was possible to ascertain, he has shown no deviation from his normal habits—when on duty he is always very busy, and when at his London flat, a very small one in Victoria, he spends most of his time at his club and with gentlemen friends. He plays a great deal of snoooker, some squash, some fives, a little tennis. He was diversely engaged every evening last week.'

'Well, well,' said Rollison, now eyeing his man with glowing admiration. 'So he didn't know Kate Lowson before.'

'It appears to be extremely unlikely, sir.'

'But someone attempted to murder him outside our front door.'

'So it appears.'

'And someone tried to kill him and Miss Lowson today.'

'Yes, sir.'

'Why, unless it's because they share a knowledge which would be extremely awkward for our Mr Thompson—such as, knowing who he is.'

'I can't imagine,' Jolly said. 'Yet, at all events, when the whole matter has had sufficient time to settle, as it were, it may be possible to make some suggestions— unless you have resolved the issue by then.' Jolly was being sententious because he was somewhat pleased with himself, Rollison knew, and probably there was more to come. 'I also took the liberty of visiting Mr Kennedy's flat.'

'Furtively?'

'Yes, sir.'

'I must tell the police. What did you find?'

'Nothing at all to suggest that Dr Kennedy is involved in this matter, nothing relating to Miss Lowson, no correspondence such as the missing letters, nothing suggesting that Dr Kennedy knows a Mr Thompson, or that he knew Mr Holmes or the late Mr Whittaker.'

'In fact,' said Rollison, thoughtfully, 'Kennedy's got a clean bill.'

'I would be extremely surprised if that were not so, although we have to face the possibility that he would expect to be suspected, and might possibly have taken all precautions to make sure that if his affairs were investigated, nothing incriminating would be discovered.' Jolly glanced at his watch, and stood up. 'It is twenty-two minutes past eight, sir. Will you change before Mr Wedlake comes?'

'I don't think so,' Rollison said. 'Switch on that tape recorder plaything of yours, keep a door ajar, and be at hand in case you think it would be wiser to have you around. No, I do not necessarily suspect Mr Wedlake,' went on Rollison, grinning, 'but I don't like him much. All right, Jolly, thanks.' He stood up in turn, as Jolly pressed a switch on the trophy wall, which connected to a microphone hidden inside a mask which the Toff had acquired in one of his cases. As Jolly turned away, and Rollison ran a hand over his hair, the telephone bell rang.

'I'll answer it,' Rollison said, and picked up the receiver. 'Rollison,' he announced, and heard Grice's voice at the other end of the wire.

'Now I really have news for you,' Grice said, quietly. 'We've had a message from the New York police, who want us to pick up a certain Maurice Holmes for murder.'

'Murder!' Rollison exclaimed.

'That's it,' Grice declared. 'An engineer working for Malling Motors' chief distributors in New York. They've sent cabled fingerprints, and they're identical with some found on Holmes's brief-case.'

'Well, what do you know,' said Rollison, heavily. 'Thanks, Bill. Anything else?'

'No,' said Grice. 'I must get off, now, I've a lot to do. But I thought this might interest you.'

'Interest,' echoed Rollison, and then heard the front door bell ring. 'I'll be seeing you,' he said, and rang off as Jolly came into the room.

'If that is Mr Wedlake, he is one minute early,' Jolly announced, and moved towards the door.

'Make sure it is Wedlake,' Rollison advised, 'I don't want any more surprises in this case.'

Jolly stepped into the lounge hall, and Rollison hesitated, wished he had a little time to breathe, then followed his man and glanced up at a periscope mirror which was fixed close to the ceiling, and betrayed anyone standing outside the front door. This was a notion of Jolly's, and had the purpose of making sure that they could not be caught by surprise.

Wedlake was there.

Three well-dressed men, two elderly and one young, were with him. Rollison stared, and Jolly stared—and Rollison thought:

'Morhead, Assen, and Bailey, the three millionaire investors in Malling Motors.' Then he saw Jolly look at him in consternation, and realised that Jolly was horrified because such guests as these should be received in a dressing-gown.

CHAPTER 20

The Three Millionaires

'Two minutes,' Rollison breathed.

'Very good, sir,' Jolly whispered back.

For his man's sake, Rollison slid into his bedroom, slipped on a white shirt with collar attached, and a dark suit, and within two and half minutes he was dressed except for shoes; leather slippers would do. During his lightning change he heard Jolly talking deferentially. There was nothing abnormal about Jolly, who had firm democratic principles, but there was no doubt that his attitude to millionaires was not quite the same as it was to lesser mortals. And Jolly was a specialist with an almost inexhaustible knowledge of Mayfair Society and the City's tycoons; he would have recognised at least two of the men on sight.

Rollison wondered what these men

would say if he calmly announced Grice's news, but he did not try to find out.

Wedlake was the largest of the four visitors. He wore a dinner jacket which was slightly too small for him, and his face was very red, his bulging neck even redder. Sir Mortimer Bailey was elderly, grey-haired, tall, painfully slim, with a nose and mouth which seemed to be set in a continual sniff. He was neatly dressed in a dinner suit of a style thirty years old. Simon Assen was an older man still, in his seventies although he might having passed for fifty-five. He had made most of his money prospecting for uranium and oil, fifteen years ago, and looked rugged enough to fit the part, with close cropped iron grey hair, a hard, tough-looking brown face, thin lips, a body which still seemed to be in perfect trim. His right hand was a false one, brown-gloved; he had lost the hand twenty years before when some dynamite he was using for blasting went off too soon. Morhead was very different from either of his companions—he looked forty, but was in fact thirty. He had inherited not only twenty million pounds but also his father's capacity for doubling money almost overnight; according to report there was no richer man in the British Commonwealth.

All three of these men had the reputation, too, of being very mean indeed with their money.

Wedlake greeted hoarsely: 'Here you are, Rollison. I want you to meet...' he named the men one after the other, and Rollison gave them a kind of communal bow, a wave and smile, and asked:

'What will you have to drink, gentlemen?'

Each man named his drink, Jolly moved to the open cocktail cabinet to serve them. Morhead and Assen studied the Trophy Wall, and only Wedlake and Bailey appeared not to take any notice of it. Rollison saw that Assen was touching the hangman's rope—which really should be round Maurice Holmes's neck, if the New York police were right.

'Rollison, I've brought the Rocket's financial backers along to re-emphasise the vital importance of finding out who's behind this sabotage,' Wedlake declared.

271

His manner seemed even more aggressive and almost overbearing; had he seen the glance Jolly gave him, even he might have toned it down. 'Everyone here stands to lose a fortune if we don't find out who's behind this soon, and if we don't make sure that the Rocket is kept secret until we're able to release it in large quantities. Isn't that so, gentlemen?'

'It is indeed,' said Bailey, and he rubbed his thin, cold-looking hands.

'Sure is,' declared Assen, dropping the rope.

'I would go as far as to say that it is absolutely essential to find out the truth of what is happening quickly,' Morhead said. He would always be a little too self-assured, a little too inclined to believe that millions made masters. 'Mr Wedlake informs us that he has offered you the sum of ten thousand pounds to ensure obtaining the solution quickly. He has our authority to double that sum.'

Rollison said: 'Generous of you.' He paused as Jolly handed the drinks round, took a brandy himself, cupped it in his hands and sniffed the bouquet. He was aware that all four men were looking at him more anxiously than they wanted to reveal. That was why he pretended to be so little impressed. 'Ah,' he breathed. 'The French knew a thing or two.'

'Twenty thousand pounds would enable you to bathe in brandy for the rest of your life,' growled Wedlake.

Rollison beamed at him.

'Possibly,' he conceded, 'but I can't really say that I've any desire to, the occasional sniff and sip suits me very well. Tell me—'

'Do you know anything else about our problem yet?' demanded Wedlake.

'A little.'

'Have you any idea who is behind it?'

'No,' answered Rollison. 'Quite honestly, no. But inspiration has been known to dawn. Tell me—'

'It is extremely urgent,' Morhead declared. 'Have you dropped everything else and concentrated on this? I could lose a fortune if anyone else learns that secret.'

'Ah,' said Rollison softly, and his lips tightened. 'That would be a great pity. One young woman has had the life choked out of her in this affair already.

273

Another was saved from death by sheer chance. Another man might die before the night's out. I'm much more interested in trying to make sure that such things don't happen again than I am in saving you your fortune, Mr Morhead.'

Morhead looked utterly taken aback. Wedlake actually opened his mouth to protest, but Assen gave a broad grin, and said:

'That's what I like, straight talk! We don't care what your motives are, Mr Rollison. All we want is to stop this leakage. Have you found Holmes?'

'No.'

'It is essential—' Bailey began thinly, in his frail voice.

'Tell me,' Rollison interrupted, 'why are you here instead of at Scotland Yard?'

The question seemed to take them completely by surprise. Assen and Morhead glanced at Wedlake, who gulped down most of his whisky and soda, looked round almost helplessly, and then spoke hoarsely:

'You're working with the police, aren't you? You brought that fellow

Grice down to Watford. We believe that you can get results more quickly than they can, and we're quite prepared to pay—'

Rollison began to smile.

'What the hell's funny?' roared Wedlake.

'Isn't it all?' inquired Rollison, with a chuckle in his voice. 'Have you been trying to buy Scotland Yard?' He saw Bailey gulp, Morhead moisten his lips, and Assen grin; Assen was by far the most likeable personality of the three millionaires. 'So you have,' Rollison said. 'They sent you away with what we know as a flea in your ear.' He chuckled more heartily. 'I can imagine what—'

'We didn't come here to be insulted,' rasped Wedlake.

'I can believe that,' agreed Rollison. 'Gentlemen, Mr Wedlake has made a common mistake. He seems to think that the word "money" has a magic which will open all doors. He's quite wrong, you know, but we needn't go into the ethics of the situation. As Mr Assen rightly said, it doesn't matter why I want to find the answers to your problems; but

I do. I don't yet know where Holmes is. I do know that a man named Bennett, an ex-employee of Malling Motors—'

'That swine!' choked Wedlake.

The three millionaires stared at him.

'The swine,' repeated Wedlake, as if the name would choke him. He turned to the three men, and went on in a shrill voice: 'He was one of our trusted employees, we discovered that he had been selling secrets, and fired him—oh, it must be about two years ago. He had associates in the factory, but we thought we'd rooted them all out. If he—Rollison! Where is Bennett? Let me talk to him.'

'He doesn't like you very much,' Rollison murmured. 'He thinks you misjudged him. He thinks that someone else actually sold these secrets. I suspect that he thinks that it was your man Holmes.'

'*What?*' breathed Wedlake. 'He's crazy! Holmes was kidnapped. He—'

'He was kidnapped, and Bennett fixed it,' Rollison agreed. 'I needn't go into details, but Bennett can't do any more damage because he's under arrest. He's made a full statement, and names a man named Thompson, a Lancelot Thompson, as being the man most interested in getting the information from Holmes and Malling Motors, and Holmes is suspected of crimes in the United States. Do any of you know a Lancelot Thompson?'

No one answered; Bailey's small and Assen's chunky head were shaken.

'I know a dozen Thompsons, we must have at least that number on the plant. What's he like?' demanded Wedlake.

'About Mr Morhead's size, he always affects a beard, he has a scar on his neck just behind the left ear,' Rollison answered. 'Sure you don't know this particular one?'

'I'm positive.'

'He seems to be the man who sold the secrets from Malling Motors, the crime Bennett was blamed for,' said Rollison. 'I don't want to make things more unpleasant than they are, but are you sure there isn't a leakage from the plant?'

'We take every possible precaution, abnormal security arrangements are laid on—it was always understood that absolute secrecy was essential, and I defy anyone to find a weakness in our plans,' Wedlake said. 'As for Holmes—what's this about a crime in New York?'

'The Yard is waiting for more news,' Rollison answered glibly.

'Someone found a weakness all right if a car was used in the streets last night,' Assen declared sharply. 'And someone knew that something big was in the wind, or there wouldn't have been this trouble with Holmes. You left Holmes too long in the States, that was your mistake.'

'I really don't see where this is getting us,' put in Bailey, and gave a nervous cough. 'The one essential thing is to find Holmes quickly, and to find out what has already been passed on to Malling's competitors. Essential, Mr Rollison, we are very worried men. We have a great deal of money involved in this unpredictable business. We readily understand that our approach to you has hardly been—ah—diplomatic, but we do ask you not to give that too much emphasis. After all, there is a very substantial export drive involved in this. A man who wishes to serve his country—'

'*Aw,* nuts,' interrupted Assen.

'I see what you mean,' said Rollison, solemnly. 'Gentlemen, I think you can take it for granted that I will do all I can and the police will do all they can—but you'll have to make sure that Malling Motors also does everything possible. If there are spies on its payroll, we want to find them.' He looked intently at Wedlake, who gulped, gave the impression that he would like to shout back, but contained his anger. 'Just one little thing.' Rollison shifted his gaze so that he could see all of the men, and could judge their expressions. 'Does anyone know a Mr Jeremiah Whittaker?'

Assen looked blank.

Morhead frowned, and shook his head.

Bailey, who must have been of about the same age as the dead man, frowned up at the ceiling, then down at the patent leather toes of his long narrow shoes, and said:

'Yes, yes. I once knew Whittaker. So did you, Wedlake.'

'So you did!' exclaimed Rollison. 'How well?'

'Not particularly *well*,' went on

Bailey, in his frail voice. 'We were among the original shareholders in Malling Motors, many years ago. Dear me, it must be *forty* years ago. Whittaker was ill-advised enough to sell out, wasn't he, ah, Wedlake?'

'Just after I joined the board,' agreed Wedlake. 'What's that got to do with it?'

'What indeed?' inquired Bailey, while the other two millionaires sensed that they were not immediately involved in this, and stood silently by.

'He was Holmes's uncle,' Rollison answered.

'What's news?' demanded Wedlake, as if he were glad to be able to raise his voice again. 'Holmes joined us because of his uncle's position at the time. Any law against that? Whittaker said he was bright, and he was bright.'

'When did Whittaker sell out?' inquired Rollison.

Wedlake began: 'I don't see what it matters, and—'

'Really, Wedlake, we must not hold back any information,' protested Bailey virtuously. 'It would be about twelve years ago, I suppose. Yes, let's say twelve years ago.'

'After the war?'

'Most certainly.'

'Thanks,' said Rollison, mildly. 'Now—'

'Well, what difference does that make?' demanded Wedlake.

'I'll tell you when I've found out,' Rollison said, 'You knew that Whittaker died a few months ago, didn't you? The unknown Mr Thompson rented his house furnished soon afterwards, as Holmes was in the United States and didn't need it. Had Mr Whittaker seen any of you gentlemen recently?'

'Really,' Bailey protested, and his pale cheeks had a faint colour, his eyes were brighter and the lids fell over them less like shutters. 'Really I think it is essential to tell you a little more. Whittaker—ah—a very astute man, a very likeable man in some ways, a very—ah—jovial man. He was however a little indiscreet. What I mean is—'

'I don't see what difference this makes,' insisted Wedlake, 'but if you're going to drag it in, make a job of it. Whittaker was an old lecher. Couldn't keep his hands away from a girl's neck-line. Used to think that if Malling Motors employed a girl, he had only to whistle and she would pop into bed with him. It got unbearable. Wife of an executive was involved, nearly a big scandal. He had to go.'

'So he didn't sell to you, he was pushed out,' Rollison said, softly.

'You could say that, yes,' conceded Bailey, judicially. 'Yes, I think that is putting it fairly. He was—ah—requested to resign from the board, and his shares were bought at what was then a fair, a very fair market price. No one was to know how Malling Motors would expand, no one was to know that within five years, his shares would have increased in value nearly ten fold. How *could* anyone be sure?'

'Did Whittaker hate Malling Motors because of this?' asked Rollison.

'Well, I'll be goddamned!' Assen breathed.

'This is quite an unexpected circumstance,' said Morhead, thinly.

'So he hated our guts because he got ten thousand pounds for shares which were worth a hundred thousand a few years later—what difference does that make?' demanded Wedlake. 'His nephew still had a good job with us, didn't he?'

'His nephew could have felt as cheated as Whittaker himself, for he would lose a substantial inheritance,' Rollison argued.

No one spoke for what seemed a long time. Finally it was Morhead who raised a white hand, looked even more pale then when he had first come in, and said:

'Are you suggesting that *Holmes* would sell this secret information? That one of the men entrusted with it had such a good reason for disloyalty? Wedlake, you must be insane. Had I even dreamed of this I would not have put a penny, not a penny, into the Rocket.'

'Well, you've sunk half a million and you stand to lose a hell of a lot of it,' retorted Wedlake. 'Holmes was as loyal as I am.'

'I daresay,' said Assen, harshly. 'But how loyal are you?'

CHAPTER 21

Alias

It looked for a moment as if Wedlake would throw himself at the older, smaller man, and Rollison was ready to stop him, if he tried. Wedlake restrained himself again, although he had gone very pale; Rollison had never seen a red-faced man change so remarkably. Morhead was staring at Wedlake, tight-lipped, Assen was glowering, and his fists were bunched; he was not going to take any attack calmly. Sir Mortimer Bailey said agitatedly:

'You know, Assen, I was fully aware of this, but it did not occur to me, it did not occur to me for a moment, that there was the slightest risk. I am sure that we can rely absolutely on Holmes's loyalty, and as for Wedlake—his whole fortune, his whole *fortune,* is bound up in

Malling Motors. One might as well suspect a man of wanting to cut his own throat. We must keep a clear perspective, it really won't help if we lose our tempers.'

'The trouble with you is that you're past it,' said Assen, disgustedly.

'Really—'

'Whatever we may think of what has happened, we're faced with the crisis,' Morhead interpolated, and turned to Rollison. 'Can you offer any hope of finding Thompson, and of making sure whether Holmes has been reliable? That is the crux of the matter. Once we know who has been working against Malling Motors, we can find out how much has been done. Except for the appearance of the one car in this street last evening, there is nothing to suggest even the possibility that a prototype of the Rocket has been made elsewhere.'

Rollison said: 'I'll have some news by tomorrow afternoon, with any luck.'

'Can you be sure?'

'You can never be sure you'll be lucky,' Rollison answered, 'but I'm hopeful.'

'We must leave it at that, I suppose,' said Morhead. 'I think we have taken up enough of your time already Mr Rollison. I speak for us all when I say that we are grateful for your help, and that we shall not be unmindful of it.'

Rollison beamed.

He let them out, Wedlake still glowering, Assen still angry. He watched in the mirror as they stood together halfway down the stairs. He grinned to himself as he turned to Jolly, who came into the lounge hall dressed exactly as he had been the previous night, complete with furled umbrella.

'I'd like to hear what happens when they're on their own,' Rollison grinned. 'Where do you think you're going?'

'To follow Mr Wedlake, sir.'

'Oh, no,' said Rollison. 'That's not the tactics at all. We're both going to wait for Mr Wedlake when he gets back to his home. Do you know where he lives?'

'He has a house on Hampstead Heath.'

'That's it,' said Rollison. 'You take a taxi and I'll take the Bentley, and then see if I'm there before you.' He crooned all that to the tune of Loch Lomond, and turned away from the door. 'Good thing I changed. We'll go the back way, Jolly.'

'I suppose it wouldn't be better for me to follow Mr Wedlake, and you to wait for him,' persisted Jolly. 'It might be wiser not to put—'

'All the eggs in the one basket,' Rollison finished for him. 'All right, Jolly, you win. Off you go.'

'Thank you, sir,' said Jolly. 'May I suggest—'

'I shall be very careful. I shall take a gun and also some of my favourite tear gas phials. I shall be armed with all my pet weapons, in fact.'

'I'm sure you are wise, sir,' said Jolly gravely.

* * * *

Rollison went out the back way, walked down the fire escape, and walked past the end of Gresham Terrace in time to see two cars being driven off, and Jolly, in a taxi, just behind them. There was little that Jolly did not know in the art of shadowing. Rollison hurried round to the garage. In the poor light, the blisters on the front of the Bentley did not show up. He slid behind the wheel, and started out very quickly. It was a little after ten o'clock—he heard a clock strike as he turned into Piccadilly. He took the almost empty main streets as far as Baker Street, and once he passed Swiss Cottage, turned off towards the Heath and went to a telephone box. He checked that Wedlake lived at a house called Ramm, and then espied a policeman walking along peacefully, and asked if he knew where the house was.

'Very well, sir, you can't miss it,' the policeman answered. 'It's facing the Heath, and you go...'

Rollison followed the directions closely, and drew up in the street next to the one he had come to find. He walked to Wedlake's house, which appeared to be quite modern, was certainly low-roofed, and, he imagined, had a wonderful position overlooking the Heath. A light was on in the hall, another in a curtained room. By night, it was very quiet—even more quiet than Park View, where old Whittaker had lived, and where Holmes had lived for a while. If Holmes had killed in New York, would he have killed again over here? The thought was ugly but persistent. Rollison let various thoughts drift through his mind, and felt fairly certain that he knew what to expect. He found a sheltered spot in the front garden, squatted on a garden seat, wished that he had brought a thicker coat—and after half an hour, saw headlights in the sky, and before long heard the sound of a car engine. Soon, the car swung round towards the house. The glow of the lamps missed Rollison, but shone on the windows. Rollison stood up and went swiftly towards the car, even while it was crunching over the gravel drive. He saw only one man. He was behind the car when the door opened, and Wedlake stopped. Wedlake slammed the door, and strode towards the porch.

He still seemed a very angry man.

'Wedlake,' Rollison called, clearly.

The man spun round. Rollison stepped into sight, smiling, the porch light shining on his face. Wedlake gaped. 'I thought we ought to have a confidential talk without the money-makers present,' went on Rollison. 'They weren't exactly all sweet reason, were they?' His words and manner puzzled Wedlake, who stood waiting for him, not scowling, not satisfied either. Rollison drew level with him and, without making the slightest attempt to disguise what he was doing, bunched his right fist and drove it into Wedlake's stomach. He heard the gush of air. He rammed his left fist into Wedlake's neck, and then his right against the heavy jaw. The big man fell back against the porch, and began to slip down, while Rollison eased the fall. Wedlake's eyes were glazed, and he was quite unconscious; conscious and fighting, he could have been a nasty customer. Rollison dragged him round to the side of the house, took a length of cord from his pocket, tied his ankles and his wrists, and then went through his pockets. He heard movements inside the house, but did not hurry. He transferred a wallet, some papers and the keys from Wedlake's pockets to his own, and then straightened up.

He went to the porch.

He studied the keys on Wedlake's chain. There were four Yales, any one of which might fit this front door. He tried two without success—and thought he saw a shadow on the frosted glass of the door. The third key slid in easily, and when he turned it, the lock went back. He opened the door, very slowly, and heard a woman call out:

'George, is that you?'

Wedlake's voice wasn't difficult to imitate.

'Yes. Won't be a minute.'

'I thought I heard the car,' a woman said, and the shadow disappeared; Rollison heard no footsteps. He pushed the door wide open, and saw a woman outlined in a doorway on the right. She was tall, rather heavily built and with a good figure. The light fell on her face, and she was quite a beauty in her rather blowsy, billowy way. She stared at Rollison as if bewildered. 'I thought—' she said.

'He won't be a minute,' Rollison said, and stepped towards her. As he reached her, he took his right hand from his pocket, holding what looked like a pistol, and said softly: 'Don't move, don't scream, or you'll get hurt.'

She *screamed*.

As she did so, she struck out at him, and he only just managed to dodge the blow. He thought he heard a chair scrape in the room. She kicked out, and he squeezed the trigger of the pistol. A cloud of gas caught Mrs Wedlake before she had time to get beyond range, and she began to cough and splutter. Rollison was no longer worried about her, for he saw a shadow as of a leaping man. He flung the door back. He heard it crash against the man who was coming. There was a cry of pain, and the shadow was suddenly a confusion of dark shapes. He stepped past the reeling woman, to see a man staggering back against the wall. Apparently the door had banged against his left knee, and he was standing on one foot and looking as if he would fall at any moment. He was a man of medium height, dark-haired, probably in the early forties. Rollison reached him, and drove his right fist into his stomach, as he had punched Wedlake. This man reeled backwards and fell heavily. The woman was gasping and trying to shout, then catching her breath. Tears were streaming down her face, and she was crouching helplessly in a small easy chair; she would be for another ten minutes.

Rollison stepped into the hall and closed the door, cutting off the sounds from the room. He heard none in the rest of the house. He went swiftly along towards a lighted room, seeing that it was an empty kitchen. When he came back, no one else had appeared, and he felt reasonably sure that the house was empty except for the couple in the big room.

He went there.

The woman was leaning back, and taking in great gulps of air. The man was trying to get up from the floor, but seemed dazed and dizzy. Rollison went to him, and the man struck out weakly. Rollison caught his wrist, hauled him to his feet, and asked roughly:

'What name are you using tonight? Mr Thompson or Mr Holmes?' When the man gasped, but made no attempt to answer, Rollison went on: 'Can you think of one reason why I shouldn't slit your throat, or choke the life out of you? As you choked the life out of June Bennett?'

Only the man's gasping answered.

Rollison turned away, and went to an elaborately carved oak bureau, where papers were spread out, and where he thought Holmes *alias* Thompson had been sitting. He saw the files from the brief-case, and in a pile under a glass paper weight some handwritten airmail letters, almost certainly the letters written to Kate Lowson.

CHAPTER 22

Missing Documents

Rollison watched the couple as he rounded the desk. A pigskin brief-case stood open near it, and inside were several more papers and what looked like small books. He took these out. The books were passports, one of them under the name of Lancelot Thompson, the other under the name of Maurice Holmes. The photographs were of the same man, although obviously taken at different times. Rollison slipped both into his pocket, and glanced through the papers. He had time to see that they were all to do with Malling Motors, and appeared to deal with design of the body and the engine. Then he saw that the woman was beginning to ease herself up from the chair, and was breathing more softly. He pretended not to notice her, nor to see that the man was also getting stealthily to his feet. His right hand was moving towards his hip pocket, too. Rollison waited until he appeared to be dipping into the pocket, then drew out the gas pistol which looked like an automatic.

'Anyone want to play "Who Shoots First"?' he inquired.

The man snatched his hand away. The woman dropped back into the chair, raising her hands fearfully in front of her.

'I thought you probably wouldn't,' said Rollison, drily. 'I think—'

Then he heard the sound of the car outside.

It was not Jolly, who would not approach so near to the house in the car. It might be one of the millionaires, or it might be the one man who was missing—the man named Bell, of whom Rollision had heard but whom he had never seen. He stood up, and the woman cringed back.

'I don't enjoy doing this,' Rollison said, half apologetically, 'but it can't be helped.' He tossed the little phial into the face of the woman, then one into the face of the man, and was quite sure that they would be helpless for at least five minutes. They took the gas in, gaspingly. The car had stopped. He went softly to the front door as he heard a door slam. He slipped into a room on the right, and saw a tall, very thin man get out of a chauffeur driven car, and recognised Sir Mortimer Bailey, who stepped straight towards the front door. Rollison waited, for there was a possibility that Bailey would have a key.

The old man knocked sharply on the door.

Rollison hesitated. Bailey was not so patient, for soon his finger was on the bell push, then he knocked again. Rollison moved from the room towards the font door, and heard Bailey mutter something angrily. Rollison opened the door, and the old man said testily:

'Must I be kept waiting for—'

Then he recognised Rollison, and broke off. At the same moment, Rollison saw Jolly, standing in the garden; obviously he had been coming towards the house when Sir Mortimer had arrived.

R-R-R-R-Rol—' Bailey began, and then stammered again: 'R-R-R-Rollison!'

'Do come in,' invited Rollison, and stood aside, opening the door wider. He glanced at Jolly to make sure that his man knew that he had been seen, while Bailey stood gaping on the porch. 'Mr Holmes-Thompson will be glad of company,' Rollison went on. 'Would you mind telling me—'

Then he heard the explosion.

It wasn't very loud, but it was unmistakable. It came from behind him, from the room where he had left the others. The doors slammed. He sprang away from Bailey and raced to it. He heard a different sound, a kind of roaring, and as he reached the door, heard Jolly running across the drive. The roaring continued. He turned the handle of the door and pushed it with all his strength, but it had jammed and he could not shift it until Jolly came to his aid. They tried together, but still the door didn't move.

'Watch Bailey!' Rollison cried, and turned and rushed out of the house and towards the window of this room. Even before he reached the corner, he realised what had happened, and saw the flickering of flames and the glow of fire. He raced towards the window, the red glow shining on his face. The fire had already taken a firm hold of the desk, and the papers on it were burning furiously. The woman was trying desperately to open the door, and seemed to be gasping for breath; at this rate she would be burnt alive. The window was long and narrow, starred with glass broken by the blast. Rollison raised his right leg and kicked out a part of the frame and some of the long slivers of glass, and climbed through. The heat was overpowering, and made him catch his breath. As he rushed through the flames, he saw Holmes-Thompson lying on the floor, face downwards; the man looked as if he had been knocked out by a piece of flying debris.

Rollison reached Wedlake's wife, and struck her sharply on the nape of the neck. She dropped into unconsciousness, and he saved her from falling, then dragged her towards the window. Near the blazing desk—in a corner which was all burning now—he opened his coat and smothered the woman's head and face, then dragged her with one arm while covering his own face and head with the other. He heard voices, and saw Jolly and Bailey just outside the window. He dragged the woman forward so that Jolly could lean forward and support her, and together they lifted her through the window.

Rollison turned round.

The flames were licking at Holmes's feet.

'Please, don't—' Jolly began, desperately.

'Use—use this,' Bailey gasped. 'Use this.' The old man had pulled a fire extinguisher from his car, and was thrusting it into Rollison's hands. Rollison saw that it was the same kind that he used on his car, struck the release pin, and sprayed the foam on to the flames near the man on the floor. Yard by yard, they receded, and soon Rollison was able to grip Holmes's shoulders and drag him, feet on the ground, towards the window. His shoes and the ends of his trousers were smouldering; whether he lived or died he would be very badly injured.

Then, in the distance, Rollison heard the ringing of a fire alarm.

'Sir Mortimer dialled 999, sir,' Jolly said. 'We shall soon have help.'

* * * *

The help arrived in less than three minutes, and by that time the woman was gradually recovering consciousness on the grass near her husband. Holmes was motionless, and Rollison could detect no beat at his pulse. Neighbours had come, some with water, some with bandages, all with good-will. Sir Mortimer Bailey looked like a gaunt scarecrow, with his face blackened and his hair singed. Rollison had no idea what he looked like, except that his face must be singed and blackened, too. The only pain he felt was in the tip of his little finger on the left hand and along the knuckles of the same hand.

His only immediate problem was what to do with Wedlake, and he did not take long to decide. Fast on the heels of the fire engine and an ambulance there came a divisional police patrol car, with a detective sergeant in charge. The only sensible thing was to tell him to get in touch with Grice, and to turn Wedlake over to him. Wedlake was also conscious, and still bound hand and foot. The sergeant recognised Rollison and obviously wanted to ask a lot of questions, but forebore.

Rollison was urged by a neighbour to go and get first aid in her house, and that was the easy thing to do. In a spotless blue and white bathroom, he saw what a scarecrow he looked, but surprisingly little hair was burnt, and his eyebrows were no more than singed. A tender spot or two on his cheeks were eased with a salve, then a middle-aged, grey-haired woman put a bandage round his hand, and ordered him to sit back for half an hour, after having coffee with a lot of sugar in it. This was the kind of treatment he had often ordered for others, and it half amused him to obey. It gave him a chance to recover his equanimity, too, and to face the unpalatable fact that someone had contrived to start the fire and to burn all the papers.

For none of those papers remained, and the whole of the big room was wrecked.

He sent Jolly out to reconnoitre and to tell him as soon as Grice arrived, and it was no surprise when Grice appeared with Jolly. Jolly was bruised about the cheeks, and looked as if he needed a bath, but there was obviously nothing seriously the matter with him.

'Well, Rolly,' Grice said, heavily. 'They tell me you've been a hero again.'

Rollison looked startled. 'I've been a *what?*'

'You saved Mrs Wedlake's life.'

'Damn it, I couldn't let her roast,' said Rollison off-handedly, and before Grice could speak again, he went on: 'How about Holmes-Thompson, Bill?'

'Dead.'

'Pity.'

'For everybody except him, I fancy,' said Grice, and sat down in a comfortable armchair, knowing that the door was ajar and that the middle-aged hostess was almost certainly at the door. 'Wedlake was conscious,' he went on.

'Yes?'

'And talkative.'

'Something had to make someone talk,' said Rollison. 'Do you know how the fire started?'

'Yes. There was another man there, who hid from you,' Grice answered. 'The man named Bell. He had instructions from Wedlake to make sure of one thing above everything else—burning all those papers. He had a small fire bomb ready for any emergency, and used it. He was one of Wedlake's mechanics years ago, and absolutely faithful.'

'Caught?'

'Picked up at Swiss Cottage, suffering from burns.'

'Talked?'

'No.'

'Hmm,' said Rollison, and frowned. He glanced at the door, as he went on: 'How much more do we know?'

'We know that Wedlake and Holmes *alias* Thompson were involved, but we don't yet know just why,' Grice said. 'Wedlake's given a garbled story about a small Italian manufacturer paying him for the secret of the Rocket, but—' he broke off.

'That doesn't add up,' Rollison said.

'You can't add, either?'

'This is no time for smart talk,' declared Rollison, firmly. 'Of course it doesn't add up. If this was simply a matter of the secret being sold out to a continental competitor, it would have been easy. Wedlake could have framed somebody else, or even sold the secret through a third party—through Bennett, for instance—and made sure that he couldn't be named. If that's his story, we aren't at the end of this case yet, Bill.'

'That's his story?'

'Talked to Bailey?'

'The old man says that after the meeting at your flat he was so disturbed in case Wedlake was involved that he came to talk to him. Apparently after they left you there was a bitter quarrel between Wedlake and the other two financiers, which nearly ended in blows.'

'I can believe it,' Rollison said, reflectively. 'Does anyone yet know why Kennedy and Kate Lowson were on the danger list?'

'Not yet,' Grice said, 'but when Wedlake has had time to recover, and when he knows that his wife owes her life to you, he will probably tell us a lot we don't know. Anyhow, he'll spend the night at the Yard. Bailey will spend it at his home, closely guarded, and you'll spend it in bed if you've any sense.' When Rollison made no comment, Grice went on: 'Did you suspect that Holmes was Thompson before you found those passports?'

Rollison had handed the passports over.

'It was on the cards as soon as we knew that Thompson had taken the Park View house, furnished—as it was Holmes's to let, and he had to give permission,' Rollison answered. 'Don't pretend you didn't suspect it, once Bennett gave us that description. Here was a man of Holmes's build and colouring, who knew Holmes's house thoroughly. There was some indication that Holmes had been held in the cellar at Park View, but none that he'd been seriously hurt. That looked like a blind to me. Obviously someone was building up a fake identity so that he could slip out of it whenever he wanted to. It had to be someone whom

Bennett would know by sight if he weren't disguised, someone Kate Lowson would know for certain if she ever saw the back of his neck with the scar uncovered.'

Grice looked puzzled. 'Scar?'

'The scar, from an old shrapnel wound,' Rollison reminded him. 'That was the explanation for the major mystery, Bill—why Kate had to be killed. She would be able to identify her Maurice from every angle, and although the scar can be concealed with powder or long hair part of the time, it shows up sooner or later. And that scar made his identity beyond all doubt. A chance meeting, even close questioning by the police, would have revealed it as an identification factor. I think we'll find that Holmes-Thompson realised that Kennedy would be bound to come round to the fact that *he* had a key to the identity. He'd seen Holmes before, of course. So had a lot of airport officials, but they weren't important. Kennedy was, the moment he became involved in the case.'

'Then Bennett was lying?'

'Bennett daren't name Holmes as Thompson, and he lied about that, but he told us about the scar to make it seem as if he was being frank,' Rollison said. 'We'll probably find that Bennett hoped Thompson would see him all right when he got out of prison.'

'I expect that's it,' said Grice quietly. 'And Kennedy had seen Holmes before, travelling under the Thompson passport.'

'Can you think of anything more likely than that he's often been to and fro?'

'No,' Grice admitted, thoughtfully. 'As they were so determined not to allow the possibility of being caught, I can't. But I can think—'

He broke off.

'I really don't wish to intrude, sir,' Jolly said, from his point of retirement in the corner of the room, 'but I feel that this is not the time for conjecture. It will be much better if Mr Rollison is able to have a night's rest, and in the morning—'

'In a minute, Jolly,' Rollison said. 'Thanks. What can you think, Bill?'

'I can think that only tremendously high stakes would explain ruthless murder like this,' Grice said, and went on very intently. 'Almost from the beginning there was cold-blooded murder. What made it worthwhile? If Wedlake got a few thousand pounds for the secret —say ten thousand—it would be as much as any small manufacturer was likely to pay. Wedlake might have felt that his whole future was in jeopardy, but—I can't see it as a motive, Rolly. Can you?'

'I cannot,' agreed Rollison, mildly. 'Peculiar how a copper and a private eye can start thinking like each other, isn't it? Do you believe Wedlake?'

'Oh, he's told some of the truth.'

'Yes,' agreed Rollison again. 'Some of the truth, Bill. And you couldn't be more right. This kind of organisation, this kind of cold-blooded murder, this premeditated laying-on of a fire to make sure we couldn't examine the documents —there's our problem.'

'Mr Rollison—' began Jolly.

'All right, all right, we'll sleep on it,' said Rollison hastily, and stood up, thanked the grey-haired woman warmly, and went out with Jolly, who had found the Rolls-Bentley, and who drove him back to Mayfair. He dozed and pondered all the way. As they entered the flat on the top floor, Rollison went through to the living-room, stared at the Trophy Wall and, after what seemed a long time, said *sotto voce:*

'What I need and what that wall needs is a Rocket, Jolly. Remind me of that in the morning, will you?'

'Do you mean that you wish to inspect one of the new cars?' asked Jolly.

'Yes,' answered Rollison. 'And there's only one place to do that—at the Malling Motors plant. And I'd like to see what the other directors look like after they know that Wedlake's under arrest.'

'It is bound to be a very great shock indeed,' Jolly observed.

'The greatest,' agreed the Toff.

He had been asleep for what seemed five minutes when he heard the telephone ringing harshly, and it would not stop. He struggled to open his eyes, and found that it was nearly daylight. He stretched out a hand for the telephone and the bell stopped ringing, but he picked the instrument up and heard Jolly announce himself in a voice heavy with sleep.

310

'Wake Mr Rollison, Jolly, at once,' Grice said.

There was a moment's pause, before Jolly said:

'Mr Grice, I do beg you—'

'It's all right, Jolly,' Rollison said into the extension. 'Hallo, Bill, what's the trouble?'

'The whole of the experimental sheds at Malling Motors are going up in flames,' Grice announced. 'I thought you might like to see the end of this Rocket.'

CHAPTER 23

Last Rocket

In the early morning, the roads were empty. A detective sergeant drove Grice's car, Rollison and Grice sat in the back, saying very little; Grice actually dozed. He had told Rollison that Bennett had admitted lying about Thompson's identity because he had believed that as Holmes, the man would see him all right, when he came out of prison.

'If I'd named him, I would have had nothing to hope for,' Bennett had said.

They were ten miles or so from the plant when they first saw the black smoke in the sky, and as they drew nearer, the smoke seemed to become blacker, and to cover a much wider area. Now and again, a fire engine roared past them. There was no need to look for signposts; they headed for the plant on the outskirts of Watford and, little more than an hour after leaving London, turned into the gates.

There were dozens of fire engines, twice as many private cars, policemen, night duty men, and tired-looking men who were obviously not used to being up at this hour, such as managers and key workers who had been summoned from their beds.

One thing became obvious immediately; the experimental sheds were absolutely gutted, and there was grave danger of the fire spreading to some of the other shops. Firemen were paying most attention to these shops; only a few damping down jets of water were being sprayed on the wreckage of the experimental sheds. The twisted girders lay about it like the charred bones of a prehistoric monster. Here and there were little heaps of wreckage, including metal which was still red-hot and hissing as water sprayed on it. There were the model cars and the prototypes, too.

On the perimeter of this scene of disaster and desolation the tall, drooping figure of Sir Mortimer Bailey stood, the upright figure of Colonel Bilston was like a statue, Carmichael and Morhead were standing together, talking in undertones, and pale-faced. Somehow, it seemed wrong that Wedlake should be missing. As Rollison and Grice studied the directors of Malling Motors, a Rolls Royce drew near the scene, a chauffeur jumped down and opened the door to Simon Assen, who stepped out, stared at the scene, and stood quite still, gaping.

Grice sought out a Watford Superintendent.

'Hallo, Bill...Very glad to meet you, Mr Rollison.' The Watford man, big, gruff-voiced, tired-looking, and with wrinkled bags under his eyes, looked as if he meant what he said. 'It's a shocking mess, but apart from holding up development, it shouldn't make much difference to output. The firemen have got it under control, they tell me. Shouldn't mean that a lot of the workers are stood off—that's the big worry at a place like this, Mr Rollison.

'I can imagine,' Rollison said.

'Any idea how it started?'

'Well, I've just had a talk with the Chief Fire Officer, very sound chap,' said the Watford policeman. 'He says that it's almost certainly arson. Two or three things point to that, including the wreckage of a car which was blown against the side of the shed, and hardly damaged by fire.'

'So there was an explosion,' Rollison commented.

'Oh, yes—two or three night duty men heard it. Only two men were slightly injured, as far as we can tell. It's going to be a big job finding out who would want to wreck a plant like this, isn't it?'

'Can't say I fancy it,' Grice agreed, and looked curiously at Rollison. 'Rolly, what's on your mind?'

'Bill,' said Rollison, and winked at the Watford man. 'I have a hunch. If it's wrong I'm going to have the biggest rocket I've ever been given—and you may present it to me.' He saw the glint of excitement in the Watford man's eyes as he went on: 'Could we collect Bailey, Assen, Bilston, Morhead, and Carmichael together, do you think? Say you want a word with them about the

Fire Officer's report?'

'Yes,' said the Watford man promptly. 'I'll fix it, but—what do you suspect, Mr Rollison?'

'Allow me my moment of triumph or of ridicule,' pleaded Rollison, and when the other man went hurrying he looked at Grice, and said: 'Any ideas, Bill?'

'I could tell there was something on your mind from the moment you stepped into the car. Why don't you stop acting like a *prima donna* before the curtain rises, and tell me what it's all about?'

'Just think,' urged Rollison. 'Why should Wedlake want to ruin his own company? Why should anyone want to destroy every prototype of the Rocket?'

'If he's being paid by a competitor—'

'Ah, yes,' said Rollison. 'Someone with more money than a small Italian manufacturer, you mean? It could be, but—ponder the facts, Bill. Think of the coincidence—the papers which Holmes-Thompson had were destroyed by fire, the whole of the experimental shed was destroyed by fire, and the little car which was used to kill Kennedy was destroyed by fire. It was always a puzzle that fire should be used as a weapon, wasn't it? Could anything have been clumsier, unless—'

'Unless what?'

'Unless it was being used to draw our attention to the fact of its existence,' Rollison said, simply, and then saw the group of directors and financiers moving off. He took Grice's arm and led him towards them.

They met in the board room in the main building, some two hundred yards from the scene of the fire. The noise and bustle seemed to fade as they entered the panelled room, their footsteps muffled by the thick carpet. Someone had made coffee, and someone had made tea.

Rollison studied each man in turn. Assen looked viciously angry, Morhead tight-lipped and cold, Sir Mortimer Bailey woebegone, Colonel Bilston rather like an officer without his men. Carmichael was sleek and polished; he took over the coffee pot and the tea.

'Superintendent, what is it you wish to tell us?' asked Bilston, stiffly, and glared at the Watford detective as if the whole of this catastrophe were his fault alone.

'It's essential that you should know at once, gentlemen,' the superintendent said, 'and at the request of Superintendent Grice of New Scotland Yard I am making it known. There is no doubt that the fire was arson, and that the research and development section of Malling Motors was deliberately destroyed.'

Bilston drew in his breath.

Assen said, raspingly: 'What's the use of standing there talking? Who *did* it? Do you know who *did* it? There were millions of pounds invested in that department, and one of the millions was mine. I want—'

'Do you know who committed this incredible crime?' inquired Sir Mortimer Bailey, huskily.

'We need to know at once,' Carmichael said. 'It is quite obvious that we were in a much further stage of development than our competitors, and that this has been done in order to hold us back. It will not only mean the risk of losing the initial investment and years of research and experiment, but it will be a deadly blow to future sales. It is the work of a rival company, of course. I find it hard

318

to believe that it is one in this country. I understand that you have detained Mr Wedlake on suspicion of criminal conspiracy. Have you yet taken a statement from him? Once we know who it is, we will have some chance of preventing them from using anything they have stolen from us in developing their own car.'

When he stopped, Assen demanded harshly:

'Has Wedlake talked?'

'Not yet,' Grice interposed.

'You've got to make him!'

'Mr Assen—'

'My God, if I could lay my hands on him, instead of leaving him to a lot of half-hearted policemen—' Assen began.

'Really, Simon,' protested Sir Mortimer Bailey.

'Gentlemen,' murmured Rollison, and although his voice was low-pitched, it made everyone present look at him. He smiled round, almost cherubic, and Grice—the only man present who knew him well—sensed that this was one of the supreme moments of his life. Moreover, Grice felt quite sure that whatever

Rollison had reasoned, or "guessed", was right; he would not behave like this unless he felt absolutely sure of himself.

'Gentlemen,' repeated Rollison, 'I don't think we need Mr Wedlake's statement. I think events speak for themselves.' He smiled into Assen's red, flushed, and angry face, and then into Morhead's. 'You two especially have been taken for a ride. I don't know about Mr Carmichael or Colonel Bilston, I do know about you. You've each put half a million pounds into this research—you think.'

There was a long pause, before the Watford detective echoed:

'Think?'

'Think?' rasped Assen. 'What the hell are you talking about?'

'Really, Mr Rollison—' began Bailey, while Colonel Bilston moved to a chair and sat down, as if all the strength had been drained from his body.

'You think you have,' repeated Rollison gently. 'You think you have helped to develop the first popular remote control and automatic collision-proof car, and the first drive-itself-with-

320

out-danger automobile—the dream car of every progressive manufacturer for a quarter of a century. But, gentlemen—there *was* no Rocket. There was no repellent treatment for metal.'

After another pause, Carmichael said thinly: 'You are talking nonsense. Superintendent, what right has this man to waste our time like this?'

'Can't say I find it a waste of time,' said the Watford superintendent.

'So you were in it, too,' Rollison said musingly to Carmichael. 'I suppose that was inevitable. And Colonel Bilston, of course.' Bilston looked as if all the blood had drained from his body, and his face looked as if he might drop dead at any moment. Sir Mortimer Bailey drew a little nearer Rollison, while Morhead demanded:

'Are you positive about this, Rollison?'

'Ask yourself,' Rollison said. 'There was one demonstration model. It was shown to you—and to everyone invited to put money into it. There was talk of other models being made—no one saw them in action. There was a small model, operated in a London street and used as a lethal weapon—to draw attention to the apparent fact that a remote-control car existed—but the model was made of a highly inflammable material which no one would use these days—unless it was intended that the car should be burned to a pile of unrecognisable debris within a few minutes of crashing.

'That car was destroyed after an explosion,' Rollison pointed out. 'The papers the police were supposed to be looking for, which Holmes—in the guise of Thompson—"stole", were also destroyed after an explosion which started a fire.

'Within a short time, all the so-called models including the prototype were destroyed here, with a fire which followed an explosion,' Rollison added. He paused, and looked into Morhead's narrowed eyes, while Assen stood with clenched fists, glaring at Colonel Bilston and at Carmichael as if he would take physical revenge on them.

'Is anyone voting for coincidence?' inquired Rollison politely. 'Because I'm not. It seemed to me quite certain that this was all part of a hoax—some outsize effort to mislead us. Once I began to think that, the rest fell into place. There was no Rocket, only a big spoof that one existed—a spoof big enough to get half a million pounds from Simon Assen and half a million pounds from Mr Morhead supposedly to finance a new model, actually to finance a company that was heading for the rocks. I think we shall find that it was depending entirely on a big American market to survive, that Holmes went to try to capture that market and failed, and that once it was known he had failed the whole of this grandiose scheme was hatched. Now we've seen them, we know that in some of his early letters to Miss Lowson he talked of this failure, and her knowledge of that could have become very dangerous. After all, a million pounds is worth a life or two.'

'One and a *half* million pounds!' exclaimed Sir Mortimer Bailey. For once he looked aggressive, and raised his clenched fists.

'One,' insisted Rollison, coldly. 'You

were only the bait. You were supposed to put up half a million, but in fact you didn't—I doubt if you have a hundred thousand pounds, you've lost too much in Malling Motors. *You* telephoned the plant, when Wedlake was captured. *You* arranged the explosion and the fire here. *You*—'

In front of his eyes, Bailey seemed to crumple up. He was in a dead faint when the Watford policeman reached him.

CHAPTER 24

Said Grice....

'Rolly,' said Grice.

'Yes, Bill.?'

'That will go down in my record as the most brilliant piece of deductive reasoning I've ever encountered.'

Rollison waved a hand, disparagingly.

'Not as good as that, Bill. Most of it fell into place once there were grounds to suspect a big bluff, instead of simple fraud. The use of that car on Kennedy really set me on the right lines. If this car was so valuable, if it were a secret guarded so zealously, if millions were invested in it, why would anyone destroy a model? It didn't make sense. I foraged around until something did make sense—which was, that someone intended to destroy it. That was only likely to be possible if it was practically worthless, so—'

He broke off.

They were turning into Gresham Terrace, still in the police car. It was the middle of the afternoon. Colonel Bilston had made a halting confession, Sir Mortimer Bailey had suffered some kind of stroke which seemed to be quite genuine, and was paralysed. Carmichael was the one director of Malling Motors who insisted that he knew nothing about it, but he was under arrest. Some of the key men in the Development and Research Division had been interviewed. They all knew that the Rocket had not been anything like so far advanced as the company had hoped; there had been failure upon failure, and the metal treatment had been kept as a closely guarded secret, talked about but never seen. The one so-called "prototype" had, in fact, been operated by electricity rather like a child's toy, and would work only on a closed circuit track. Some progress had been made with a remote control mass production car, but nothing remotely approaching an automatic evasion car had been developed. One or two small models which could be controlled by a man standing fairly near had been built, and one of these had been used in Gresham Terrace—operated, it was believed, by the man Carby, who had been on the payroll of Malling Motors as a test driver.

The police car slowed down.

'Coming in for a cuppa?' invited Rollison.

'No, thanks,' said Grice. 'My desk will be piled ceiling-high by the time I get back to the office. But don't get out for a minute.' He turned so that he could face Rollison, and went on: 'I mean exactly what I say. It was a brilliant piece of deductive reasoning. You get better as you grow older. The remarkable thing is that once you'd pointed it out, I could see how inevitable it was, how inescapably right all the way through. Holmes daren't let Kate Lowson live because she might see that scar on the back of his neck—he couldn't keep it covered all the time—and when questioned about the letters she would reveal the early failure in America. Once the police even suspected that he had been the mysterious "Thompson" the danger would be deadly. He had to vanish because of the New York murder, and it's almost certain according to the New York police reports that the engineer he killed knew what he was doing, and blackmailed him. So, Holmes had to disappear, and Thompson take his place. As he'd been running a double identity, that wasn't difficult, but there were complications. Kennedy ran into trouble because he was at the airport at the unfortunate moment, and the woman fascinated him.' Grice paused, just for a moment. 'Holmes couldn't wear his beard at the airport, so couldn't avoid recognition, and Kate Lowson had to be prevented from seeing him,' he went on. 'June Bennett could identify him as Thompson, and of course she didn't tell her brother because he thought he was working against Malling Motors.' Grice pushed a hand through his brown hair, and smiled faintly. 'Well, I suppose I ought to stop telling you how right you were. What do you think will happen with Malling Motors now?'

'I think that Assen and Morhead will

take the firm over,' Rollison answered, lazily. 'The whole plant has been riddled with inefficiency and corruption for a long time, it needs to be completely re-organised. I certainly can't see Assen letting his money be thrown away. There's one other thing that could be checked, Bill.'

'What's that?'

'Whether old Jeremiah Whittaker died of natural causes or was murdered. It wouldn't greatly surprise me if he found out something which gave him an idea of what was going on, and he had no reason to love Malling Motors. He might have told his nephew to drop it, or take the consequences.'

'I'll have it checked,' Grice promised. 'Not that it will make a lot of difference, now that Holmes is dead.'

'The truth can be good for its own sake,' murmured Rollison. 'Bill, thanks. I'll leave you to your paperwork.' He shook hands, got out of the car, hurried up the stairs whistling to himself, saw the door open as he reached the top step, and thought: 'Jolly gets better every day, not I.' Jolly was smiling, for he had been told what had happened by telephone.

'Hallo, Jolly,' Rollison greeted. 'I shall take the rest of the day off.'

'I hope you will see one more caller, sir,' said Jolly, and stood aside, so that for the second time Mike Kennedy appeared in the Toff's flat in front of the Toff's eyes when he wasn't at all expected. He looked pale but rather dark under the eyes, but those eyes were bright and eager, and there was a lot of power in his grip as he took Rollison's hand.

'How's Kate?' inquired Rollison.

'She's all right, thank God! I took her to her flat and left her there; she shouldn't do too much for a day or two. She can't wait to see you and thank you, Rolly. And my God, to think I once thought you were a blow-hard!'

Rollison chuckled.

'You wouldn't have surprised me as a murderer, either. I'll come over later in the day and see Kate—just in time for a drink before dinner, say.'

'Wonderful! I—er—there's one other thing,' went on Kennedy, with a kind of fierceness to his grin. 'I did lift something from 40, Park View—you were right when you suspected that I had a guilty conscience. Where's that parcel, Jolly?' He turned round and led the way into the big room, picked up a brown paper parcel from the desk, and handed it to Rollison, adding: 'It won't go off, I promise you that.' He watched Rollison unfasten the string and unwrap the contents—and there, in tissue paper, lay a big, dark false beard and moustache.

'How's that for the Trophy Wall?' he demanded.

'That couldn't be better,' Rollison said, and picked it up, examined it closely, and then handed it to Kennedy. 'You hang it up,' he said. 'Choose any place you like.'

Kennedy studied the wall, then put his head on one side, climbed on a chair, and fastened the beard and moustache immediately beneath the top hat with a bullet hole through it—the trophy which had the highest place of all.

THE END

331